And then, as if sensing his mood, the singing started. It was the same as before, spectral children's voices curling out of the echoing tunnel like smoke.

'Oh, don't deceive me. Oh, never leave me . . .'

Preston had never in life or death felt anything like it: it was like a cold stone in his gut that spoke with certainty of unimaginable horrors . . . he felt as if the tunnel, or something inside it, was watching him, waiting to see what he would do.

Preston Oldcorn finds himself in a desolate void – trapped in the chasm between life and death. Discovering that he is not alone, he must stay one-step ahead of his enemies and unlock the mysteries held by this new world as he tries to save his soul.

But doing so means braving the darkest and most feared part of town:

COLD BATH STREET

COLD BATH STREET

A. J. Hartley

Illustrated by Janet Pickering

uclanpublishing

Cold Bath Street is a uclanpublishing book

First published in Great Britain in 2017 by
uclanpublishing
University of Central Lancashire
Preston, PR1 2HE, UK

This edition published 2018

978-0-9955155-8-1

1 3 5 7 9 10 8 6 4 2

A CIP catalogue record for this book is available
from the British Library

Printed and bound in Great Britain by Clays Ltd, Elcograf S.p.A

This book has been typeset and designed by
Brionee Fenlon and Sam Johnson and copyedited
by Josh Moorby and Laura Collie

To my family: past, present and future.

PROLOGUE

Preston, Lancashire, England.
15th September, 1978.
9:22 p.m.

Preston Oldcorn lay quite still, eyes tight shut, trying to shrug off the cold grip of the nightmare. He'd had it before, but this time had been different. Worse.

It hadn't been so bad at first, he had merely relived a part of his walk home from Scouts, trudging alone along the dark pavement with its high hawthorn hedges and its pale and over-spaced street lamps. On Woodside Avenue he had paused to take in the way the light behind the tree made its clutter of bare branches spiral like a cobweb. He passed the top of Heather Grove, then turned toward Ribbleton Avenue and Greenlands. The dream replayed

1

all of it down to the last detail, even the part about his Scout uniform.

Preston hated the Scouts. All that standing to attention, marching around, and practicing knots, like they were soldiers. He especially hated the uniform which always had to be pristine, the red and white neckerchief rolled just perfect so the leather woggle slipped up to his throat like a noose. Some of the boys were proud of it, the same boys – oddly – who despised their John Southworth school uniforms, but Preston felt stupid and embarrassed in it. This very night, just as he was leaving Woodside Avenue, he had passed a family standing outside a house with a For Sale sign. There was a man leaning on the bonnet of an off-white, rust-spotted Vauxhall Cavalier, a woman with a furrowed brow, and a girl close to his own age – maybe fourteen – with chestnut hair and bright, clever eyes. Her parents looked weary and dissatisfied, and Preston caught the woman saying something about the kitchen being too small. The girl just looked bored. Preston had tried to give her a sympathetic look as he passed but she had smirked and said, "Nice uniform."

Preston had wanted to roll his eyes and shake his head, make some quick, smart remark, that said he knew how ridiculous he looked, but instead he had flushed and looked away, saying nothing. As usual.

It wasn't the uniform's fault, of course. He would have done the same – which is to say he would have done nothing – no matter what he had been wearing, but it still rankled. He was nearly fifteen, for God's sake. Girls looked at him sometimes. He could tell. He just couldn't respond, couldn't stop being a kid. Now, if he had the leather jacket he'd been saving for, the one his father flatly refused to let him buy, then maybe things would be different. Maybe *he* would be. The jacket would mean Preston was a rebel, not a punk exactly, despite the music he had started listening to over the summer. It wouldn't mean he was a delinquent, just that he was his own person. He didn't see why his father couldn't see that. It was time his parents got out of his way. Time they accepted that he wasn't a kid anymore . . .

All that part of the dream had been real: the walk, the girl, the thoughts about his uniform and the leather jacket. It had all happened just like that, which was strange when he thought about it, because dreams weren't usually so realistic. They jumped around, following their own surreal logic, leaping from place to place, turning people into other people, the mood rolling like the grey waves on Blackpool beach. Not this one. This one had been just the same as his walk home, every ordinary and uninteresting detail just the way it was every Friday night.

Until he crossed the street.

Then it had changed. Without warning, the flat, drab recreation had tumbled into nightmare. Preston had waited to cross over the road, staying as long as he could in the glare of the newsagents, passing Cuffs, which sold the best ice cream in town, the Spinning Wheel, and the hardware shop that always smelled of paraffin, because the other side of the street was dark and shrouded with trees. But then he had come to the cemetery railings and the other side of Ribbleton Avenue had quickly become the lesser of two evils. So he crossed, heading for home down Stuart Road, as the world slid towards dread and horror.

There was an unnatural darkness at the bottom of the street, down by the tree-shrouded cutting where the old railway line ran. Preston felt it like damp, like fog, a darkness deeper and more menacing than the heavy shade of the chestnut tree by the tracks. He had glanced away, trying not to look, focusing on turning the corner onto Langdale Road, thinking about what he would say to his father about the leather jacket, but then he saw it and his thoughts derailed.

It was nothing more than a grey shape at first, a pale shadow not quite as deep as the darkness which stood in the silent gardens and blank windows of the sleeping houses, but he felt its presence and his heart quickened with his footsteps. Still, when he looked back again, it had halved the distance between them, and though Preston broke into a faltering run, it closed impossibly fast. The anger he had tried to maintain over the jacket evaporated. He stared fixedly ahead of him and dashed for the street lamp at the top of Langdale Road. But now the shadowy figure was somehow in front of him, between Preston and home.

His heart throbbed and a bleak and breathless chill descended on him.

It was her, the Bannister Doll. He was sure even though she was not quite as he had imagined her before. Her hair was long and wild, but her face seemed to flicker like there was something darker and stranger behind it. Her skin was pale, bluish as if she had been caught in a storm or drowned in deep, cold water. But it was the eyes that stopped him, for they were colder still. They were terrible, black, and full of a malice so hungry that for a moment Preston thought they were less like eyes and more like mouths.

The ghost looked at him with those awful, ravenous eyes, and then it did something new, something Preston had never dreamed before. It stretched an insubstantial hand toward his chest. He looked down as he felt the cold pressure of the spectre's fingers easing through his breast pocket, and Preston caught one more strange and unfamiliar detail; she was barefoot.

He wasn't sure what happened next. One moment her hand was no more than chill night air reaching into his body, and the next it was real: hard and cold and closing around his heart. There was a rush of sudden and unbearable pain, and a lunging panic that opened his eyes and mouth as wide as they would go. Then everything had gone dark.

How much time had passed since the nightmare had finished, he didn't know.

Now Preston lay quite still, waiting for the memory of the dream to slip away, his eyes still closed, conscious of a confused unease that wasn't fading, that was actually getting stronger and more pronounced as he regained his waking senses. Something was wrong still. He remembered leaving Scouts. He remembered the walk home and, however much he would prefer to forget it, he remembered the ghost nightmare. But there was a gap in his memory between the walk and the dream. He did not recall getting home, pushing through the back door into the kitchen, or going to bed. He didn't remember seeing his parents, or sullenly arguing about why he should be allowed to have the leather jacket. He tried to find these things in his head, but there was nothing, no sign any of them had ever happened. There was only the walk, and the ghost dream.

With a dragging sense of horror, he forced himself to open his eyes.

He should have seen the soft glow of his bedroom window, and caught the silhouettes of the old model Spitfires and Hurricanes he had suspended from the ceiling years ago, but there was only a dark sky and a fringe of black leaves. He was outside. The pavement was cold and hard beneath him, gritty and damp under his fingers. He was in the street a block from home, the very place he had dreamed of.

But it had been no dream. He had never reached his house, his parents, his bed. The attack had been real, and as Preston placed an unsteady hand on his chest, he realised that his heart, which should have been thumping with fear and panic, was quite still, was – in fact – not beating at all.

At fourteen years, ten months and five days old, Preston Oldcorn, was dead.

CHAPTER 1

But Preston couldn't be dead. He was thinking. He was conscious. He was no vague, spectral mist, but solid flesh and bone. He pressed his knuckles against the tarmac and both were hard and substantial as ever. He stood up and took a step. His footfall sounded loud in the still night. He began to walk towards home, and everything was quite normal. Or almost everything.

The night was unusually quiet. Silent, really. He glanced back up to the high street but Ribbleton Avenue, which should have had at least an occasional car, was utterly, uncannily, still. There were no cats padding gingerly across the street, no movement of trees or even any impression of a breeze. There were no flickering televisions in the windows of the houses, no sounds of radios drifting through the night, no squabbling, no parents yelling to their kids to keep the noise down, in fact no noise at all, no sign, indeed, that there was anyone but him alive on the surface of the earth.

Or not alive.

Preston began to run. He crossed Stuart Road in the long diagonal he always used and rounded the corner onto Langdale, the little street where he had grown up, moving at a full sprint. He knew each broken patch of tarmac, each root-bulged splitting of the pavement beneath his feet, but tonight it all felt off somehow, wrong. He passed the O'Brien's place, the Morris', the Patel's, the Dolan's. He reached the brick gateposts of number six, and turned up the side of the house, past the old pear tree, fumbling in his pocket for the key.

He grasped the cool metal door handle, slid the key in and turned it, and there he was, in the tiled wash house which had, until last year, been a coal shed. One more door and he was in the kitchen.

"Mum?" he called. "Dad?"

No response. He tried the lounge, where they might be watching television, but it was empty. Everything in the house was as it had been when he had left it, but it felt different, deserted like a reconstruction in a museum: a house where no one actually lived. He ran upstairs to his own room and it too was just as he had left it, the old Spitfire model on the window ledge, the crucifix on the wall, the scattering of books by the bed, his battered guitar propped up in the corner, and the stool draped with the school uniform he had cast off only hours before. He peered out into the darkened street below and saw no movement beyond the looming shadow of the pear tree, no lights in windows, no signs of life anywhere.

Preston sat on the bed struck by a swelling grief and horror which crawled out from under the blanket of confusion which had wrapped him. He could not argue it away. It made no sense and defied everything he thought he knew or believed, but he was dead. He was sure of it. The world was the same, but he was alone in it. Perching there on the edge of his bed, pretending he was waiting for his parents to come home after a late meeting, he began to cry. He wept for a full minute before he noticed that his eyes were still dry, and that realisation, strange and unsettling as it was, silenced him.

How long Preston waited for something to happen, he couldn't say. He had pushed the display button of his brand new digital watch repeatedly but the little red numbers lit up the same way every time: nine twenty-two. It had apparently been damaged in his fall. Or so he thought until he checked the alarm clock in his bedroom and found that it had stopped at the same time. He went down to the kitchen to check the battery clock over the table which made the radio crackle every seven minutes, but it also read nine twenty-two. So did the oven clock and the one on his mother's bedside table, this last checked cautiously with the hope that she might be sound asleep in there. The room was bare, the bed had not been slept in, the clock stuck dead on nine twenty-two. Preston paced the silent house for what felt like an hour, then considered making something to eat but decided that he – curiously, unusually – wasn't hungry. Finally, with nothing better to do, he went out into the back garden.

He squeezed down the side of the garage and through the hole in the hedge which put him at the bottom of Moorfield Drive, where an apple tree and two tall poplars grew, and then walked up through the silent houses to Ribbleton Avenue. At the top of the road he stopped and listened but the silence was absolute: no cars, no barking dogs, no lights in windows. It was like he was still dreaming, and that sense of being outside the real world gave him a rare flash of defiant confidence: he shouted into the night.

"Hey! Someone. Is anyone there?"

He turned, scanning the houses for lights coming on or doors opening, still bellowing. He called for the police. He experimented with swear words he usually kept to himself, now bellowing them in the hope that the neighbourhood would awake out of sheer outrage. He screamed about his parents for not letting him have a lousy leather jacket even if he paid for it with his own money. He ranted about the Scouts. He called his teachers everything he could think of. Soon lights would go on. A window would open and someone would demand his name or threaten him with arrest, and it would be glorious . . .

Nothing happened.

He finished his shouting and the night fell silent again. He felt for his heart drumming inside his chest but could still feel nothing. Though he could hear and see as normal, and his body felt the same as it always did, the world had changed. For a long moment Preston just stood there, numb, then he turned right and walked a few hundred yards. He crossed Cromwell Road and then Ribbleton Avenue itself, standing for a long, silent moment in the middle of the road, looking in both directions, but feeling unnervingly safe. No headlights in either direction, no sound of distant traffic. He could lie down in the middle of the road if he wanted. He didn't. Instead, he turned into the darker, tree-lined street where his grandmother lived: Woodlands Avenue.

It was at her house which backed onto the cemetery, the graves of which were just visible over the wall if you stood on the radiator in the back bedroom, where he had first played with the idea of doing the Bannister Doll ritual. He had heard different versions of it from Gez and the kids at school, but everyone agreed that if you called on the Bannister Doll and held one of those green glassy pebbles which they put on graves, you'd see her. The idea had fascinated and appalled him. Why would anyone want to do that? Why did he, except to prove to himself that he could?

He had never done it. But the Doll had found him anyway.

Preston reached the house on Woodlands Avenue and opened the gate. The echo of the passage between the house and the garage and the rolling sound of the sliding door which admitted him to the back were so familiar, so utterly real and concrete in his mind, that for a moment it seemed impossible that anything strange had happened. It felt ordinary. Normal. But he had no heartbeat, and when he wept his eyes stayed dry. Though his body felt solid enough, he was growing sure that by now he should be feeling hunger, tiredness or the need to go to the toilet. He didn't, and in his gut he felt sure it wasn't right. The back door to his grandma's house was unlocked, which was not unusual, but inside it was exactly as he had known it would be: the same as always, but dark, silent, and empty of people.

He moved from room to room, calling, but it was as if everyone had been scooped out, everything else left untouched: the newspaper by the armchair in the sitting room, the bread knife on the kitchen table beside the enamelled tin bread bin, the pots in the draining rack. He should have been able to smell the bowl of sliced cucumber in malt vinegar which his grandmother prepared to go with the Sunday salad, or see his grandfather, paralysed down one side by a stroke years before, mashing the bread flat so it would slot into the toaster, but there was no one. The house felt gloomy and abandoned. Melancholy. Back upstairs he settled on the edge of the bed in the back room which overlooked the cemetery and stared blankly out.

So this, he thought, was death. Or rather a kind of half death. He considered the old idea that babies who died before baptism went into a sort of nothing which existed between Heaven and Hell but was not Purgatory either. Limbo. Purgatory was where your sins were purged in time so that you could move on to heaven, but babies could commit no sin, so there was nothing to be purged. They had no faith, they had done no good deeds, and they had not been sacramentally bonded to the Church, but neither had they deserved damnation. So they went to Limbo to wait for the ending of the world.

Or something like that.

He wasn't sure he really believed it. In fact, he didn't know that anyone his age did anymore. It was one of the bits of church held on to by the old ladies who went to mass everyday, by the priests, and by some of the teachers. Ordinary people didn't still think like that, did they? What kind of God would leave a baby hanging in nothingness because it hadn't been baptised? It didn't make sense.

And yet here he was, neither saved nor damned, not obviously being purged of anything, but stuck in this strange nine twenty-two no place. Maybe none of it was true, he thought, with a worried pang of anxiety, of guilt, but maybe this really *was* Limbo and he had somehow found his way here even though he wasn't a baby. Maybe his life had been so bland, so empty of either real sin or real goodness that he had been left here forever. Maybe if he'd told Gez Simpson what he thought of him, maybe if he'd punched him in the mouth and told the Scoutmaster what he could do with his uniform and his knots, maybe if he'd bought the leather jacket for himself regardless of what his parents had said, or – better – stolen it right off the rack in the shop, maybe things would be different. Worse, perhaps, but maybe not.

Preston gazed out of the window to the graveyard as his unease turned into something sadder and simpler like loneliness.

He wasn't sure what he had expected, though he thought perhaps that if he was a ghost then the cemetery might seem different to him, but it looked the same as it always did. He stared at it, and then, without warning, he felt a surge of excitement. Someone was moving through the headstones. A boy not much older than himself.

Preston ran.

* * *

In seconds Preston was down the stairs, out of the house, down the garden and up against the cemetery wall, but from here he could see nothing of the graveyard.

"Hello?" he said, his voice low.

"Who's that?" called a voice from the other side of the wall.

"It's . . . my name is Preston Oldcorn," said Preston. "What's going on? Where is everyone?"

"What ya whispering for?" said the voice, closer now. His accent was thicker than Preston's. "There's no one to wake up on your side of the wall or mine." The boy laughed, a grubby, throaty sound which Preston wasn't sure he liked. "You know what's going on, mate," said the boy. "You just haven't got used to the idea yet. So. You coming over or what?"

"Over?"

"Over the wall," said the boy on the other side.

Uncertainly, Preston reached for handholds on the wall but his fingers couldn't get a grip. In fact, he couldn't touch the wall at all. The air seemed to thicken as he reached for it, becoming solid and unyielding several inches from the mortared stone blocks. He peered at the wall and tried again but though he could see it quite clearly, he couldn't reach it.

"I can't," he said. "Why can't I?"

"'Ave you ever climbed the wall before?" asked the voice contemptuously, as if the answer was obvious.

"No," said Preston.

"Then you won't be able to now, will ya?" said the boy. "Probably never came in the cemetery did ya?"

"I did," said Preston, defiance swelling in him. "I'm an altar boy. I come to the graves at funerals."

"Ooo," mocked the boy, "'ark at him. *Were* an altar boy, you mean. You'll have to come round the long way. I'll meet you at the cemetery gates."

"When?" said Preston, torn between apprehension and relief at being able to talk to someone, anyone.

"Soon as you can get there," said the boy.

Preston retraced his steps, leaving his grandmother's house, then running through the still silent streets up to the cemetery where the evening's bizarre events had begun, driven by the need to know what had happened, and what he was.

Were an altar boy, you mean . . .

He ran all the way, getting faster as he realised that he felt no tiredness, and when he stopped it was as if he had been sitting for hours.

"Boo," said the boy, leaping down from the high wrought iron gates. "I can still haunt you even if you're a ghost an' all."

The boy was perhaps seventeen, with dark curly hair and laughing green eyes. He wore old-fashioned clothes of thick cloth with large buttons, and heavy-looking shoes.

"You're new," he said, poking Preston in the chest with a grimy finger. "What got you, car?"

Preston shook his head.

"Not sure," he said.

"That's 'ow it goes sometimes," said the boy, wisely. "Still, dead's dead, innit?"

Preston shrugged. He didn't want to ask, didn't want to seem ignorant or desperate, but he couldn't keep the question in.

"I really am dead?" he said, his voice faltering.

"Kind of," said the boy. "Merely Dead, not most Sincerely Dead."

"What?"

"Not like the witch in *The Wizard of Oz*."

"What?" said Preston again, annoyed.

The boy hunched over and sang in a squeaky, nasal voice, "*That she's not only merely dead, she's really most sincerely dead*!"

He cackled with laughter.

"What's the difference?" asked Preston.

"Merely Dead means not alive, but you aren't Sincerely Dead until you've passed on."

"To what?" asked Preston.

"You tell me," said the boy. "You're the altar boy. Maybe angels and demons, saints and what 'ave you. Maybe it's just like this only with people. Or maybe you come back as a greenfly or some'at. Or maybe there's nowt. You step through the door and pouf! Gone. Like you never were. No memory, no feelings, no name." He leered as he said it, guessing that Preston would be stricken with dread at the thought. "Not worth the risk, is it? So I stay here: be my own man. They call me Roarer."

He drew his grimy hand from his pocket and held it out. The two smallest fingers were missing, the wound ragged and open but bloodless. Preston hesitated.

"Dogs," said Roarer simply. "It don't hurt none. Don't heal, but it don't hurt."

He considered it, as if noticing the damage for the first

time, and Preston thought he caught the pale gleam of bone just before Roarer offered his hand again.

Reluctantly Preston shook it and said his name.

Roarer laughed his grubby laugh again.

"You really called Preston? Like the town?"

"Yeah," said Preston, grudgingly proud of the effect this seemed to have on the other boy.

"Bloody odd name," said Roarer. "They call you that in case you forgot where you lived?"

"Funny," snapped Preston, affronted. "I've never heard that one before."

"All right, all right," said Roarer. "Keep your 'air on. Gonna have some fun, you and me, *Preston*. Do as we like 'ere with no one to say otherwise. You'll wish you'd died sooner."

Preston managed a smile, but he wasn't so sure.

"Wanna go sing rock and roll songs in church?" said Roarer. "Or steal stuff from Marks and Spencers?"

"Like what?" Preston asked.

"Anything you like," Roarer returned with an expansive grin. "Everything's free to us, new boy. No one here to catch us is there? Want to play football for Preston North End? On the actual pitch, I mean. Right where Bobby Charlton and Tom Finney played. Preston playing for Preston! Take all our clothes off and play naked if you want."

"Why would I want to do that?" asked Preston.

"Because you *can*," Roarer concluded. "See? The world of the Merely Dead is, as they say, your oyster, mate."

"Huh," said Preston, nodding. He grinned, though not quite as expansively as Roarer had hoped.

"Not what you expected, huh?" said Roarer, and his smile had a touch of understanding, even compassion, so that Preston shook his head though he said nothing. He hadn't expected anything. Not really. Never really thought about it. Death was for other people. Old people. But this . . . How could it be this?

"Cheer up," said Roarer. "It's not so bad. Could use a little more LIGHT," he added, shouting the last word at the sky, then shrugging apologetically. "Always worth a shot," he said. "But seriously, it's alright here. And everything you were ever told about death is wrong. Even the words are wrong. *That Roarer*," he said, putting on a pompous voice, "*has passed on*. No, I've not. I'm still 'ere. They just can't see me. *He's kicked the bucket! He's joined the heavenly choir*. There is no choir, dead or alive, that would ever have me, trust me."

And so saying he burst into a rendition of "God Save the King" so awful and off key that Preston couldn't help but laugh, even if some of that was gratitude at Roarer's effort.

"But . . ." Preston began.

"What?"

"What about my family?" Preston said, embarrassed.

"Best if you forget 'em," said Roarer, kindly, "or at least put 'em out of your head. You'll want them to remember you, of course."

"Why?"

"Keeps us anchored, like," said Roarer, "the memory of the living. If they forget you completely, you sort of fade. I think. Anyway, I figure the trick is to keep people talking about you. If they're scared of you, they can't forget you, can they?"

"Are the living scared of you? I've never heard of you and I've lived here all my life."

"Well I've not been gone long, have I?" said Roarer, put out. "I'm working on it. I'll be around for centuries, me, long after you've turned to mist and vapour, you see if I'm not."

For all his bluster, Roarer looked uncertain, even anxious, so Preston redirected the conversation.

"But how can you scare people into remembering you if there aren't any people? I haven't seen anyone but you since I . . . you know . . ."

"Snuffed it?" said Roarer. "Seeing the living takes practice. I can do it, nearly anyway, when I want to, like. But it's not easy."

"How do you do it?"

"Oh, you have to, ya know, really want to see them," he said, airily, avoiding Preston's eyes. "And you have to focus your mind and whatnot."

"You can't do it," said Preston.

"I can too though, right?"

"Let's see it then."

"I'm not gonna do it now, am I?" said Roarer, as if no suggestion could be stupider. "Not now."

"You can't do it," Preston repeated, disappointed.

"You'd better watch it," said Roarer, balling his fist and holding it close to Preston's face. "Just 'cause you're dead doesn't mean I can't knock your teeth in." He hesitated and then lowered his fist. "I can see the living. Sort of. I done it twice. I'm just . . ." he hesitated and dropped his eyes, "not sure 'ow I did it. I was thinking about my sister, and everything got a bit lighter and I could almost see the world of the living, only it was sort of fuzzy, but then it just went away and I was back 'ere. I keep trying but . . ."

"Maybe your family forgot you," said Preston.

Roarer turned a furious glare on him and for a second Preston thought the boy really would hit him. Then he looked down, shaking his head, but saying nothing.

"Come on," said Preston at last. "I'll show you where I lived."

* * *

25

Ironically, the thing which had been able to reach into Preston Oldcorn's chest to stop his heart could not enter the house where he had lived for the same reason that Preston had been unable to scale the cemetery wall. Being older and more expert than Roarer, however, it could watch the house with its still living inhabitants and it did so almost lovingly, waiting for a glimpse of the people whose lives it had wrecked. Because Roarer was half-right. Ghosts last longer if they can retain a foothold in the world of the living, and most survive by being bound to them by the thin tether of memory, of love and, if neither of those survives, of fear. But for those spectres whose powers are greater and who can affect the world of the living as few ghosts ever could, even fear is only a tool. What sustains them is determination, a singularity of purpose bound to their recollections of what they once were, and for a few this becomes a consuming and altering obsession.

The thing which had killed Preston Oldcorn lived on grief. It had no name. Not anymore. But it thought of itself simply, as The Leech. It sucked life from those it destroyed, and though it felt a rush of wild joy when it killed, its principle sustenance came not from murder but from those the dead left behind. So the Leech targeted only victims whose absence would leave a hole in the hearts of those who survived: family, friends and – most particularly – parents.

The Leech had stumbled on the truth of this long ago. The feelings people had for adults who died unexpectedly were often as confused as they were potent, but for children, the grief was purer, richer, a clear and uncomplicated well of loss and despair which thrilled the Leech to its splintered soul and gave it power. Preston Oldcorn's parents wept and held each other, speechless for days, their lives collapsing, and in its heart, the Leech crowed with bitter joy and triumph.

But the Leech did not just kill the living. It had a use for the dead as well, a purpose both strange and terrible which was suited only to ghosts, a purpose besides which mere dying seemed like nothing. The anguish of Preston's parents would sustain the Leech for a little while but soon, very soon, it would find the spectral remains of the boy himself and then . . . then Preston would truly know terror and despair. The Leech pictured him in his Scout uniform, the horror in his eyes . . . This was one of those cases where the hunt would be almost as pleasurable as the final, dreadful act itself.

CHAPTER 2

Preston wasn't sure how much time had passed. His digital watch – along with every clock he could find – still read nine twenty-two, and though he was alert for any change in the world around him, none came. The soft darkness of the evening never lifted and morning never arrived, but it seemed that he and Roarer spent days exploring the empty town together, pausing only when they reached a place that one of them had not been in life or where, for reasons they could not explain, they seemed to be seeing different buildings. Sometimes it seemed that Preston slept, a curious, dreamless sleep from which he could remember nothing, and from which he woke uneasy and unsure of where he was. Each time he had to remember what he had become, so that for all his play with Roarer he got used to feeling an unspecific sadness tugging at the edge of his mind.

But he felt no pain, no tiredness, no hunger. He didn't have to stretch or scratch or go to the bathroom. His body did everything he wanted it to as efficiently as it ever had, and it did so without slowing, so he could sprint for miles, laughing as he did so. Doors opened for him – so long as they were places he had been in life – something Roarer proved by taking him to Cuffs' the confectioners on Ribbleton Avenue and saying, "Help yourself!"

Preston stepped into the tiny deserted shop and gaped up at the huge jars of pear drops, sherbet lemons, chocolate éclairs and bulls eyes that were stacked across the wall behind the counter. He gave Roarer a look.

"Help myself?" he said.

"It's not like you're stealing," said Roarer, climbing onto the counter and considering the sweets. "This isn't the world of the living. Everything here is for us. Good eh? So what do you fancy? Sarsaparilla drops? Liquorice Allsorts? Dolly Mixtures?"

"Chocolate," said Preston, grinning, and considering the individually wrapped Mars bars and Curly Wurlys.

"What are you waiting for, Christmas?" asked Roarer, popping the cap of a jar and grabbing a handful of dark red sweets. Preston laughed, chose a Bounty, and tore the paper off.

They spent a good twenty minutes sitting on the glass-fronted counter sampling the merchandise, and Preston was too delighted by the fact of what they were doing to be bothered by the truth that none of the sweets really tasted of anything. He giggled as Roarer tried and failed to smoke a pipe he had stuffed with tobacco, laughing as the other boy struggled to draw the smoke into his lungs.

"No breath," Roarer concluded. "Can't smoke without breath."

For reasons Preston couldn't explain, this struck him as uproariously funny.

"Come on," he said at last. "I want to go other places."

Those other places were at St. John Southworth's school, which both boys had attended, though they seemed to have had different teachers. They ran all the way there and then pelted through the empty corridors shrieking at the tops of their lungs in deliberate violation of every school rule they could think of. They sat on the headmaster's desk and scribbled nonsense words all over the blackboards. They raided the tuck shop for more sweets, but the pleasure was more in the thrill of breaking in than it was in the eating, and most of the flavourless sweets got discarded and forgotten. They played football in the gym, deliberately blasting the ball at the high windows until one of them popped in a shower of glass and they cheered. From time to time, Preston found himself listening for the sound of irate teachers coming to reprimand them, and when he remembered that they were completely alone and safe he would crow like a rooster with delight.

Roarer led him to a pub – the Plough at Grimsargh – and both found that having visited with their families years before they could get in, which meant they could pour themselves beer and sit in the corner with pint glasses in front of them like adults. Roarer pretended to be the barman, pulling pint after pint, and little shot glasses of gin and whisky from the optics behind the bar. The alcohol tasted of nothing and had no effect on them, but that barely dampened the delight of doing things that would have got them into serious trouble in life, so much so that they stayed there for hours. Roarer built up a fire in the hearth, and though they couldn't feel its heat, it pleased them to watch the flames as they sampled their flavourless drinks.

"See," said Roarer. "Told you we were going to have fun."

"Is this just our world, you think, or is it the same as the one living people are in?"

"What's the difference?" Roarer said, shrugging and sipping his pint. He was standing at the bar again, leaning with adult nonchalance as if Preston might have forgotten that the beer in his glass wasn't really beer at all, not to them.

"I mean, you said there are living people here. We can't see them and they can't see us, but they're here. So we're in the same place but not in the same time?"

"Time?" said Roarer. "What's time got to do with anything? We're here. The world of the living is here an' all. So?"

"You think there are people here now?" asked Preston. "Living people? In this place, I mean, but in the . . . you know . . . *present?*"

"The Living world, you mean?"

"Right."

"Try and see," said Roarer with a half-mocking shrug.

"Now?"

"Yeah. Just focus on this place and try to, you know, see what it's like on the other side."

"How?"

"I don't know. Imagine it. Course, if it's too hard for you . . ."

"I'll try," said Preston, feeling defiant. He sat still and closed his eyes. Roarer giggled. "Shut up," said Preston. "I'm trying to concentrate."

"You can't do it," said Roarer. "Not by trying. No one can."

"Shush," said Preston.

And as he said it, he squeezed his eyes even more tightly shut but kept in mind the room with its roughly plastered walls and the blackened oak beams hung with horse brasses, and then – without really knowing why or how he was doing it – he reached out with his mind, feeling for life – real life – in the world beyond. He didn't notice how quiet Roarer had become, but gradually he became aware of something else, a low, droning sound that mounted in volume like a plane going overhead. He opened his eyes.

He was sitting exactly where he had been by the pub's fireplace, but there was no fire lit now and there was no sign of Roarer. The room was lighter than it had been, though it was also indistinct, like he was looking at it through thick bevelled glass. The droning sound seemed to be coming from the main bar. Preston stood up carefully, conscious that his senses were strangely muffled, and stepped into the open doorway. The bar was similarly light but its details were smudged and shifting, and for a moment Preston thought it was also deserted. But then the sound altered, grew closer and he saw the flickering outline of a middle-aged woman in jeans, bent over the vacuum cleaner she was pushing across the carpet.

Preston stared, then started to wave and shout, but his own voice sounded distant and echoing, barely audible over the Hoover, and the woman did not look up. Almost immediately he felt a sudden and overpowering exhaustion, unlike anything he had felt since he had died, and he sank to the floor in a heap, his eyes closing.

When he opened them again he was back in the dimly lit pub with Roarer who was staring at him with eyes wide, a look of wary admiration on his face.

"You crossed over, didn't you?" he gasped.

Preston still felt fuzzy, but he managed a nod.

"You did," said Roarer. "Just like that! Wow. One minute you were here and the next you just sort of faded away, then you came back, only over there! And you really saw the living? You must be like a ghost superhero or some'at. What was it like? What did you see?"

Preston had to find the memory before he could relate what had happened.

"Cool," said Roarer. "I'm gonna try."

Preston watched him sleepily as he took up the same position and closed his eyes tight shut, but nothing happened. After a moment Roarer opened one eye and looked around, frowning, then repeated the process again. Three times he tried, with no effect, and when he gave up the last time he was surly.

"What do I want to see the world of the living for anyway?" he concluded. "I'm mighty fine right where I am."

They left the pub and set off walking back towards Ribbleton along the old railway line, Preston watching Roarer as he balanced along one of the rails, arms outstretched whistling what sounded like Jailhouse Rock between his teeth.

"We have to walk everywhere?" he asked.

"What, you think there are ghost buses just for us? Nah. Shanks's pony for the likes of you and me Preston, lad."

Preston brooded.

"Where does this line go?" he asked at last.

"Through Grimsargh all the way to Longridge in that direction," said Roarer, nodding back the way they had come.

"And this way?"

"Into town," said Roarer. Preston was sure the boy avoided his gaze as he said it.

"What?" he said.

"Nowt," said Roarer.

"There is," said Preston. "Where does it go?"

"I said," Roarer replied, warningly. "Town."

"So what's the big deal?"

Roarer looked away irritably, like he wasn't going to say anything, but his pride was pricked and when he turned back to Preston his face was wooden, giving nothing away.

"No *big deal*. Goes to town. Through the Miley Tunnel." Preston had heard dark stories associated with the tunnel, but he was unprepared for the way Roarer said it, like he was scared even of the name of the place.

"Which runs where?" asked Preston.

"To the station," said Roarer. "Eventually. Goes down by Cold Bath Street."

Again there was the hint of evasion, as if there was something the boy didn't want to talk about, and Preston was about to make some teasing remark when he saw movement up ahead. He stopped, gazing along the track. It was a man with a lantern.

Preston stared, pointing.

"Look!" he gasped.

Roarer just kept walking as if nothing could be less interesting.

The man was pacing the railway line which ran through a short and gloomy cutting. As the boys got closer, Preston could see that he was dressed in antique overalls and wore a heavy moustache. His eyes were cautious, anxious even, and at first he did not seem to see the two boys as they approached.

Preston gaped at him, but when he turned to Roarer the other boy just shrugged.

"You knew we weren't the only . . . ?" Preston began, though he stumbled over the word 'ghosts.' "You knew he was here?"

"The Brakeman's always here, isn't he?" said Roarer, unimpressed. "He never leaves this spot. But you won't get anything interesting out of 'im."

Preston frowned and approached the man who was shuffling along the track, his oil lamp held at shoulder height.

"Hello?" said Preston.

The man's eyes seemed to flicker towards him momentarily, but he said nothing and continued his slow trudge along the line, checking a large pocket watch as he did so. Preston fell into step beside him.

"Are you working?" he asked.

"'Ave to check the line before the ten o'clock train," said the Brakeman without looking at him. His voice was low, gruff and rich with local accent. "Check the brakes on't wagons, check that the points are set, check the wagon loads are stable."

He recited the tasks slowly, mechanically, as if afraid he might forget something.

"What's your name?" asked Preston. "I'm Preston. That there's Roarer, though I don't suppose that's his real name."

"Check the brakes on't wagons," said the Brakeman, "check that the points are set, check the wagon loads are stable."

"Yes," said Preston. "I'm sure you will. But what's your name?"

"Name," the Brakeman echoed vaguely.

"Yes," Preston urged. "Your name. What are you called?"

The Brakeman's eyes glazed, becoming even more distant, and then – speaking in a deep voice and enunciating each syllable carefully – he said "Child killer."

Preston took a step back.

"What?" he gasped.

But the Brakeman was already losing his focus.

"What do you mean?" Preston asked.

"Check the brakes on't wagons," the Brakeman said as before. "Check that the points are set, check the wagon loads are stable."

Preston was almost relieved that the ghost said nothing else.

Child killer . . .

"Told you," said Roarer, when Preston returned to him. "Barely knows you're here. He's always like that. *Check't wagons. Check't points.* Just ignore him."

"But why is he stuck?" Preston wanted to know. "We're not."

"He's been here longer," said Roarer, avoiding Preston's eyes. "He's forgotten everything else."

"But why?"

"How should I know?" said Roarer. "Something to do with how he died, I expect."

"What happened?"

"He died," said Roarer with an expansive shrug. "An accident of some kind. He was supposed to stop the train and he didn't, or something. He got killed. So now he checks all the stuff he didn't do properly the day he died. So what?"

"And there are other ghosts in other parts of the town?" asked Preston.

"That there are," said Roarer, "but you're best staying out of their way."

"Why?" asked Preston, trying to sound like he didn't care one way or the other.

"Just trust me," said Roarer. "You don't want to meet them. Most of them are like this. Stuck in a loop from the past. But there are one or two . . . Like I said. You don't want to meet them."

"Why not?" Preston pressed. "It's not like they could do anything to us. We're dead like them."

Roarer glanced down and his face was uneasy, even scared.

"Dead, yeah," he said, "but not like them."

"What do you mean?" Preston asked, but Roarer just looked away, trying to hide the expression on his face.

"Just leave it," he muttered. "There's dead like us or the Brakeman – Merely Dead, right? – and there's Sincerely Dead, when you move on to whatever. But then there's other stuff. Bad stuff you don't want to hear about. Some ghosts can do things to you. Horrible things. Especially to kids. And not just little kids neither."

Child killer, Preston thought.

"Kids?" said Preston. "You mean live kids or . . . ?"

"Ghosts like us," said Roarer, less and less comfortable with the subject. "Some ghosts stay like the Brakeman but there are kid ghosts that just disappear."

"Maybe they pass on," said Preston, ignoring the anguish in Roarer's face. "Maybe they become Sincerely Dead and . . ."

"No!" said Roarer, angry now. "Something takes them. Something worse than regular ghosts."

"What happens to them?" asked Preston, not wanting to hear.

"I don't know," said Roarer, "but if you see any, in a group, like, you stay out of their way."

"A group of dead children?" Preston asked. He didn't feel so cocky now. He had thought he was safe here, that the worst had already happened and that whatever the limitations of the place, there was at least nothing to fear.

"They *look* like dead children," said Roarer tightly. "But they aren't. Not anymore."

"They're not dead children?"

"They are," said Roarer, tense now, hating to have to spell it out. "Or they were. But now they are something else."

"Maybe they can be saved," said Preston. "Helped to move on."

Roarer gave him a disbelieving stare.

"Just stay out of their way," he said.

"Are they connected to the Brakeman?" asked Preston. He didn't know why, but he didn't want to repeat what the Brakeman had said people called him.

"The old railway bloke?" scoffed Roarer, his good mood returning. "Check the points and what have you? Nah. He's harmless."

Preston frowned again and kicked a stone.

"What about," Preston began, stealing himself to say the name, "the Bannister Doll?"

Roarer turned on him, his eyes haunted, and Preston saw that his panic and fear had returned with still greater intensity.

"Don't talk about her, all right?" he said in a rushed and anxious whisper, half-covering his mouth with his ravaged hand. "Never. Don't even mention her name."

After that he wouldn't speak, and the two boys drifted away from each so that when Preston stopped to study the nettles growing by the tracks, Roarer wandered out of sight. After running aimlessly around for what felt like an hour, Preston gave up looking and didn't see him again for what seemed like many days.

* * *

Preston should have known it would be the Bannister Doll which would get him, and not only because of the dreams. He should have known because in his heart he knew he deserved it.

It had been going on for weeks. Preston's patrol leader at Scouts was called Gerald – Gez – Simpson. He went to the same school as Preston, and they were in the same year, though Gez was two sets below Preston in every subject so they didn't interact much there. Gez wasn't your common bully. True, he would punch you hard on the arm if you stepped out of line during inspection, and jab your breast pocket with a hard finger if he thought you didn't have your first aid kit in there, but he always worked within the law and never once got into trouble for the atmosphere of dull dread and anxiety which he managed to maintain in his seven boy patrol. The little kids – Stephen Cummings in particular – were terrified of him.

"Scare the little 'uns now and you'll have 'em for life, right Preston?" Gez had said once. Preston had sort of nodded and grinned, saying nothing, doing nothing. He felt cowardly for it, but Preston was – as his father liked to point out – a man of few words, and he disliked confrontation. Gez never actually hurt the little 'uns, not really, and Preston told himself they could stand a little toughening up. Probably stood them in good stead later, he added, pretending he didn't sound exactly like his dad when he said it.

Though much of his bullying was the usual – looming over them until they winced and then hitting them for not standing to attention, the casual mockery which always contained the threat of a beating if they objected – Gez's real gift was for storytelling. There was always time to squeeze in a little horror during the end of patrol gatherings, particularly if they were outside in the dark, and Gez had worked it up to a fine art, revelling in the horror which he spread among the younger kids like a contagion. He had a whole storehouse of gruesome tales of psycho axe men, vampires and other assorted nonsense, but he got his best results with ghosts.

He had been telling stories about Chingle Hall, near Goosnargh. Preston had been there during the summer, but though there was supposed to be the ghost of a monk who made the rooms cold and moved objects around, he had found the place interesting rather than scary. In Gez's practised and inventive hands, however, the medieval house became a chamber of various made-up horrors in which the floors ran with blood. On this particular night, Stephen Cummings kept taking off his glasses with unsteady hands to wipe his eyes, and the young Scouts had all looked spooked. Preston had hoped vaguely that something would redirect the conversation, but it didn't, so he just sat there, listening, watching Gez grinning wolfishly at him as the three youngest boys went to pieces.

It was lurid, self-contradictory nonsense, but the little kids didn't know any better, and Gez served it up with a straight face, loving their mounting terror, feeding off it. It was cruel, but Preston didn't like to argue with Gez, and it wasn't like Preston was scared of the stories.

Except one. He didn't know why the Bannister Doll frightened him so much, particularly since Gez's account varied every time and was clearly no more factual than his other yarns, and was mostly bits of old horror films cobbled together. Sometimes the only element which was consistent from one telling to the next was the name of the ghost itself, but that was enough. The dead girl's ghost had wormed her way under Preston's skin as if in punishment for his not protecting the younger boys against Gez's other assorted ghouls.

So now his death at her cold, pale hands seemed like destiny, as if his cowardice had let the Doll in, first to his head, then – quite literally – into his heart.

He should have told Gez to shut up whatever the consequences. And then he should have gone home and told his parents that he was done with Scouts once and for all, however much the uniform had cost, that he didn't want to 'build his character' or 'learn some responsibility.' And then he should have informed them – calmly, deliberately but, with sure finality – that he was buying himself a new leather jacket. But he hadn't done any of those things. Instead he had given into the dragging need to keep his head down, to do what was expected of him, an idea he wore like the chain wrapped around the ghost of Jacob Marley in that Christmas book his mum read every year.

So Preston had listened to Gez's tale of the Bannister Doll who had been brutally murdered – how, varied with each telling – and now sought vengeance on the living. It should have been stupid, but Preston's dreams put a face to Gez's story, one which waited in the shadows, followed him through sleep with slow but inexorable purpose . . .

"Have fun passing the grave yard," said Gez to the little kids, laughing in the way he copied from the Hammer horror films.

"It's okay," said one of the other boys to Stephen Cummings once they were all out of earshot of the patrol leader. "There's no such thing as ghosts."

The little boy nodded blindly, not believing it, and when he looked at Preston for encouragement, his eyes shining and desperate, Preston had turned away, managing to return Gez's grin, showing which side of the joke he was on.

And for that, that split second of cowardice and backhanded cruelty, she had, only minutes later, taken him.

* * *

It hadn't been a decision to return home. It was just where Preston's feet took him. Indeed, he had a nasty feeling that his options were getting fewer. Many times he had found himself with nothing to do and nowhere to go and had drifted back to the empty, silent house on Langdale Road, and now he feared this was becoming more than habit. He was forgetting some of the places he had gone in life, and as he forgot, they closed to him and ceased to exist. To test the theory he took a detour, stepping into the driveway of number seven, across the street, a house where Jimmy Higgins had lived until his family moved back to Liverpool two years ago. Preston had been in the house many times, though not recently, and he had given it no thought since his watch had stuck at *9:22*.

He tried the front door and it opened, but stiffly. He moved into the kitchen, but found it strangely blank, like an unfinished painting in which the artist hadn't got round to the details that made it a real place where people lived. Worse, the air felt thick so that moving across the room required real effort. It was an unpleasant feeling, like being trapped in something that was hardening around him, and he felt a sudden panic, that if he didn't get out it would seal him in like a prehistoric mosquito fossilised in amber. He turned and pushed his way through, but once outside he tried the door again to see if it was easier this time. It wouldn't budge. Preston stared at the door but found that he could no longer picture what was behind it.

He remembered Roarer's remark and wondered with another twinge of anxiety if he was forgetting the world, or if the world was forgetting him.

"Have to focus," he said to himself. "Have to concentrate. Stay alert. Keep reminding yourself of everything."

But it wasn't easy. Nothing demanded his attention. He didn't have to eat or sleep, so there was nothing around which to structure his time, nothing to give his existence a sense of purpose. Concentration alone wouldn't do it. He needed a mission, preferably something that would shine some light on his own situation.

"The Brakeman," he decided.

There was something about the old railway worker that Roarer didn't know. Preston was sure of it, some detail to the man's story that was central to why he was still stuck among the Merely Dead. And if he had to guess, he'd say it was connected to what the Brakeman had said in that rare and momentary second of lucidity: child killer.

Maybe if he could explain that then maybe, just maybe, Preston could discover how to set the Brakeman free. And if he could do that for the railway man then perhaps he could figure out how to do something similar for himself. More to the point, he half-admitted to himself, focusing on the Brakeman meant he wouldn't have to think about the Bannister Doll.

Not yet, anyway.

He paced every room of what had been his house before settling in his usual armchair in the lounge in front of the cold gas fire, and a thought occurred to him. He got back to his feet and crossed to the bookcase, scanning the spines of the books until he found what he was looking for on the top shelf, a battered hardcover bound in stained and faded red cloth: *A History of Preston*. Maybe there would be something there, some clue to events of the past that would help him understand what the Brakeman needed from the present.

Preston reached for the book, but his fingers found only a curtain of dense and unyielding air such as he had discovered in Jimmy Higgins's kitchen. He tried to press through it, but could not reach the book. Even in his own house some places were, apparently, closed to him.

He ran his hands over the mantelpiece and felt the objects there: his mother's Beatrix Potter figurines (Peter Rabbit, Duchess, Foxy Whiskered Gentleman), a glass vase of dried grasses and flowers, and a brass carriage clock (nine twenty-two). He tried the books on the lower shelves (a road atlas, a dog-eared paperback on astronomy which talked about landing on the moon as something which might happen one day in the future, and another on dinosaurs, portions of which he had once known by heart) and all came out easily. But when he reached for the top shelf again, it was like trying to push his hand through glass.

He sat back, weary and miserable, staring up at the history book's red spine, eighteen inches and a lifetime away. And then an idea struck him. He couldn't look at the book because he had somehow never reached up there in life, but the book wasn't just there in his world. It was almost certainly still in the same place in the world of the living. If he could reach into that, into a slightly different time but the same place . . .

He had done it before in the pub. Perhaps he could do it again. Perhaps he could get to the book, open it, read it not in his own moment, but in whatever came next, in the future from which he had been removed.

Not the *future*. The present. His nine twenty-two

moment was a bubble in time, in what the rest of the world knew as the past.

And maybe Roarer was right. Preston's ability to see the living present might be a kind of gift, a spectral super power. He might be able to use it to help other ghosts who, like him, were trapped in their moment of death.

But he was getting ahead of himself. He quietened his mounting excitement and focused on the book on the shelf in front of him. That was the first step.

He got to his feet again, but this time, instead of reaching only with his hand, he reached with his mind, imagining the same space in the living present. His eyes closed and he mouthed silent words.

"I need that book. I need it. I *need* it . . ."

And suddenly aware of his future in this dwindling world, the idea became true to Preston in ways it hadn't been before. The book was a toehold in a reality which had slid forward without him. He reached for it like he might reach for the trailing rope of a boat he had fallen from, straining desperately for it as the boat moved off, its passengers and crew unaware of him splashing in its wake.

He reached . . .

Grabbed . . .

Preston opened his eyes and the room was different.

It was light. Again it was fuzzy, like he was looking

through a misty window, but it was day-lit and full of colour. Somewhere outside he could hear the drone of traffic. The clock on the mantelpiece read half past four. Elated, he stabbed at the book with his fingers and touched it. It felt somehow soft, yielding, but it had substance. Carefully and with a tremendous effort, he closed his thumb and forefinger around the top of the spine and tugged. It shifted fractionally, but then his fingers slid free, and the light in the room flickered.

Preston gritted his teeth and concentrated harder still, reaching for the book, and this time when he plucked at it, it slid two whole inches out of the shelf before his grip melted.

He reached up once more, straining against the wave of exhaustion he felt growing in his head, but just as he touched it there was movement to his left. He turned and saw a figure in a blue dress positioning a photograph on the mantle above the gas fire.

Mum?

He forgot the book, and that part of the room immediately fell dark and insubstantial. Only his mother shone pale and clear as she touched the photograph tenderly. It was a picture of him taken at his birthday party a year ago. Preston saw her face, her shining brown eyes fixed on the picture, and he reached for her as the room collapsed in around him. His fingers strayed to her hair, and he leaned forward as if he was lifting a tremendous weight, but as she withdrew her hand from the picture, his strength failed. The room shrank into blackness, his mother vanished, and Preston collapsed in grief-stricken exhaustion.

* * *

Preston woke – if that is the right word – alone in the dark house on Langdale Road. He felt disorientated and, though he had no way of telling for sure, he felt he had been unconscious for a long time. He had never felt so tired, but there was a warmth inside him, like a glow around which he had curled up. His mother. He had seen his mother, not in a memory, but as she was in the living present.

As she *is*, he told himself.

And if he could do it once, draining though the experience had been, he could do it again.

Just not now.

The exhaustion in his mind was almost physical. Those excited thoughts about saving ghosts by means of his special ability leaked out of him and he felt only weary and alone, capable of nothing but lying exactly where he was. He had no idea how long he stayed in that position but thought that it was, at the very least, several hours, though he had no way of knowing if it had been more.

Preston found Roarer sitting on top of the cemetery gates, one of his favourite haunts as it had been, he said, when he was alive. Roarer was good company when he was in the right mood: full of jokes and a wild, animal energy that sent him whooping and bounding through the night with a thoughtless abandon that Preston could never quite match. Together they ran tirelessly for miles and miles, moving at sprinting speed like deer and laughing at the easiness of it. Preston had always hated running, especially the dreaded cross-country run around Cow Hill at school, but now it was easy, and having someone to share the delight of it made it better still.

But at other times, Roarer would become suddenly quiet and sulky, prone to lash out if probed, and Preston learned to leave him alone until he felt more sociable. Sometimes it seemed like an age before their paths crossed again, and the interim became tedious for Preston, leaving him depressed and lonely. After such spells of isolation, he would be overcome with delight at meeting Roarer again, though he sometimes thought the boy's black moods were coming more frequently and lasting longer.

They squabbled about music. Preston hummed snatches of Elvis Costello songs and Roarer gave him odd, quizzical looks which got deeper and more derisive when Roarer heard the singer's name.

"There's only one Elvis," said Roarer, who then launched into a medley of 'Hound Dog,' 'All Shook Up' and 'Jailhouse Rock.' He gyrated into the empty middle of the road, pivoting on the balls of his feet and waggling his hips.

"Only one Elvis," he concluded, happily. "Elvis 'The Pelvis' Presley. Who's this Costello character?"

"'I Don't Want to Go to Chelsea?'" Preston tried. "'Watching the Detectives?' 'Pump it up?'"

Roarer just shrugged.

"He's the best," said Preston, thinking back to an episode of *Top of the Pops* only weeks before he had died when he had gotten his mother to confess that there was something compelling about the singer in his odd, too small trousers and oversized glasses. Preston loved the whole thing: the look, the clever words, the edge to the music. It was like the songs were written for him. If he had the nerve, that was who he'd want to be. But he could no more pull off an outfit like that than go to the moon. That was why he had fastened onto the black leather jacket worn by JJ Burnel, the bassist for the Stranglers, who he had seen on the telly snarling out '5 Minutes,' his bass slung low around his hips. The jacket was what he needed. It was tight-fitting, all studs and zippers, and it hissed attitude and toughness and a flippant, disreputable confidence that . . .

"Sounds dreadful," said Roarer. "Not like real music at all, is it?"

"I'm going to see the Brakeman," said Preston, keen to change the subject.

"Suit yourself," said Roarer stepping out into the middle of the road and lying down. Even though there were no cars, it looked odd, recklessly brave which – Preston thought – was probably the idea.

"You coming?" he asked.

"Nah," said Roarer, closing his eyes. "I'm comfy here, thanks."

"Fine," said Preston, annoyed. "I'm not just going to sit around. I have to do something."

"Like I said," Roarer answered, his eyes still closed, "suit yourself."

Preston hesitated, then started walking away, half-hoping Roarer would call him back or come jogging to catch up, but when he didn't, Preston felt he had no choice but to keep going. He walked all the way up past Partington's where his father had bought their old Ford Cortina, past the library and the long climb up to Gamull Lane. There he cut down to the railway line and picked his cautious way through the darkness to the cutting where the Brakeman was walking his endless patrol.

"Hello," he said warily.

The Brakeman did not seem to notice him.

"Check the brakes on't wagons," he said to himself, "check that the points are set, check the wagon loads are stable."

"Remember me?" Preston tried again. "We talked before. I'm trying to find out who you are. You don't remember, do you? Not really."

". . . check that the points are set, check the wagon loads are stable."

"Yes, I know you have to do that," Preston insisted, stepping deliberately into the patch of amber light cast by the Brakeman's lantern. "But I thought that if we could figure out who you are, or were, I suppose, then maybe . . ."

"Check the brakes on't wagons," said the Brakeman, oblivious.

"Listen to me!" said Preston, his voice rising with sudden frustration. "You're dead! The trains on this line don't need you checking loads and points. Where you are now, there aren't any trains."

". . . check the wagon loads are stable."

"What wagons?" Preston shouted bitterly. "This is stupid. You are wasting your time. There's no reason for you to still be here so just stop! You can probably – you know – move on. Die for real, get out of this meaningless little bubble and, I don't know, meet God, or rest, or . . . something. Anything would be better than this!"

"Check the brakes on't wagons," said the Brakeman.

Wondering why his temper had risen so quickly, Preston stared at him, then tried a different tactic.

"Why do they call you child killer?" he demanded.

There was a sudden, cool silence. Very slowly the Brakeman swung his lantern up high and took a step towards Preston, his eyes wide and staring. Preston stood his ground, but he was suddenly scared, and wished he had dragged Roarer along for company.

"Children," said the Brakeman, musingly, in that low growl of a voice he had used once before. "Children."

Preston stared at him, but even as the plural word stirred terrible thoughts – not the killer of one child, but several, many even – he felt his own fear dwindle. The Brakeman's eyes were not mad or hostile. They were sad, so sad, in fact, that if they were still capable of tears, Preston knew they would be overflowing. For a long moment the Brakeman stood frozen like that, his face a mask of grief and horror, and then it faded and he went back to his imaginary tasks.

"Check the brakes on't wagons . . ."

Preston nodded, backing slowly away, and then turned and headed down toward Cromwell Road.

"That's how it is with some of them," said Roarer, who Preston finally found climbing a tree in Ribbleton Park behind the Hesketh Arms. "They forget everything gradually."

"But he was worse this time," said Preston, throwing gravel chippings into the long grass. "There's something about the day he died which is keeping him stuck there."

"That's why you've got to stay on top of things," said Roarer, tapping the side of his head with his mangled hand. "Like me. Don't let anything slip away. That way you keep track of time and don't forget yourself."

"Time," Preston echoed, glancing at his useless watch. "But how can you tell how much time has passed?"

"Have to stay alert, haven't you?" said Roarer. "You don't need a clock if you can feel everything."

"I suppose," said Preston, uncertain. "Your hand," he said, framing a question he had wanted to ask many times about how the boy had lost two of his fingers. "Did it happen before or after?"

"After, obviously," said Roarer. "Wouldn't look like this if it happened before, would it?"

He stuck his hand under Preston's nose so that he could see the torn flesh and sinew around the sockets.

"And it doesn't hurt?" Preston asked, unsure why it mattered.

"Nope," Roarer said. "Didn't even know it had happened at first. I'd only been dead a day or so. I was just fightin' 'em off – the dogs, I mean – and one of 'em got hold of me. I ripped me 'and out and thought I'd done something right smart, you know?" he continued, laughing at himself, "'til I saw the bloody hound still 'ad two of mi fingers in its gob! Thought about going after it to get 'em back, but that would have been too stupid even for me, wouldn't it? And then I got to thinking about what being Merely Dead would be like if they ripped one of mi legs off, or tore mi eyes out or something and I took off like I was in the Olympics. They came after me, ran for miles – fast, too, like wolves – but I lost 'em down by the river."

"Were they real dogs?" asked Preston, suddenly aware that he had seen no more animals than he had people. "I mean, living?"

"Nah," said Roarer. "Ghosts, like us. Their teeth feel real enough though."

"Dogs can be ghosts?"

"Why not?"

"Can other animals be ghosts?"

"I saw a ghost cat once," said Roarer, as if considering this for the first time. "And I've heard of ghost horses. But they usually have riders. But ghost cows and chickens and sparrows and what not? Nah. I reckon there's got to be a strong link to people. Dogs are man's best friend, right?" he said, as if this proved the argument.

"They don't sound too friendly," said Preston, who had always had a terror of large dogs, particularly in groups and running wild as they did sometimes around Moor Nook.

"They're like the Brakeman," said Roarer. "After a while, they forget everything about who they were except for one thing, and they hold on to that so that everything else goes away. It's like madness. Dog ghosts wander by themselves a bit, but eventually they meet other dog ghosts and it's like they go back to the way dogs were a million years ago or some'at. So that all they remember how to do is hunt. 'Course, there's not much for them to chase except each other," he said with a grim little smile, "and us. They don't need to eat of course, but they'll chase you down and tear you to bits anyway, 'cause that's all they know how to do."

Preston tried to laugh as if it was funny or merely interesting, as if the idea of the ghost dogs hunting him didn't fill him with terror.

"So, how long is it since you . . . ?"

"Died?" said Roarer, grinning. "What, you scared of the word even though you are already dead?"

"I'm not scared of it."

"Sounds like it."

"How long?"

"Since I snuffed it?" Roarer mused. "A month. Maybe six weeks."

Preston frowned, considering Roarer's old-fashioned shoes and suddenly remembering his rendition of the national anthem.

"Why didn't you sing 'God Save the Queen'?" he asked. "The night we met. Why did you sing 'God Save the King?'"

"Never got used to singing *Queen*," said Roarer with a shrug. "Feels wrong, you know?"

"Got used to it?"

"Yeah," said Roarer. "It was always 'God Save the King' when I was little. So I sang that. So what?"

"What year is it?" Preston asked, avoiding the other boy's eyes.

"What?"

"You've been dead a few weeks, right?" Preston pressed. "So what year is it?"

"1958," said Roarer, as if nothing could be more obvious. "Why?"

But Preston didn't answer. He was backing away, then turning up to Blackpool Road and breaking into a full run. Roarer thought only weeks had passed since he died, but Preston knew for a fact that the boy he had been playing with had been buried at least twenty years ago.

And if Roarer, who prided himself on being alert to his predicament, could be so terribly wrong about just how long he had been out of the world of the living, then what did that mean for Preston? Had he only been dead days, as it seemed, or was it months, years?

He ran for home.

* * *

The house looked the same as ever but then, he reminded himself, his watch said it was still nine twenty-two. Things could have changed dramatically in the world of the living and he would be no wiser. He stepped into the lounge, because that was where he had done it before, and he focused on the bookcase by the gas fire. He isolated his need to see what the living present looked like, and holding that thought like a light in front of him, he closed his eyes, and strained with all the energy of his mind.

Again, the long stretching reach, like he was trying to snag the end of a rope in water . . .

He heard the dragging roar of traffic before he opened his eyes. It was morning, and the room was full of soft, angled light. But it was not the room he knew. The book detailing *A History of Preston* was gone, and the bookcase was different, shorter, and filled with unfamiliar titles. The pictures on top were of children he had never seen before. The flock wallpaper he remembered his father hanging had been stripped and the walls painted a pastel green. The shag carpet had been replaced by something with tight and geometric patterns on it and the net curtains at the windows were now stylish swags of lustrous fabric. Gone too was the boxy brown television set with its greenish screen and radio-dial knobs, replaced by something sleek and black with a little red light in the corner. There was no picture of Preston on the mantle.

The strangeness of the house, the way it spoke of another, later age quite unfamiliar to Preston struck him like the blow of a hammer. It hadn't been days or weeks. It had been years since Preston died. He could just tell, and now his parents were gone, perhaps dead, but Sincerely Dead, moved on beyond where he could ever see them again.

The world shimmered and began to darken, but Preston fought it, wrenching it back into focus as he left the lounge and climbed the stairs to his own room – or whatever the room would be in this strange and uncertain present. He knew before he stepped in, but it was still hard to take in the pink and purple walls, the unrecognisable pop star poster where his British Birds identification chart had hung over the bed, the books and makeup where his lovingly painted model planes had once been.

He blundered out, and this time as the light and colour started to slide, he could not force it back into focus, and when he tried the exhaustion fell upon him like a great black wave. He collapsed on the landing, without the energy to hold back the grief which overcame him.

His home, his family, were gone. He was truly lost and utterly alone.

And there was a girl in his room.

CHAPTER 3
OCTOBER 1980

Tracey Blenkinsop – the girl with, she said, the stupidest name in recorded history – sat in her bedroom and looked down into the front garden. Her parents had cut down the pear tree, or rather, they had paid some men with a truck to do it for them, and now the view from the window was so different that it felt as if they had moved house again. Tracey had liked the tree, or rather she had liked the way its thick green top blocked her window completely so that if she positioned herself just right she could look out and see what seemed to be an impenetrable wood. But her father said the roots were coming up under the house and prying the bay window in the lounge away from the wall. She wouldn't miss the wasps that gathered around the fallen fruit, or the sappers who nipped in on their way home from school to steal from it, but the thought that she would never smell the soft and fragrant pears again as they came ripe filled her with an unexpected sense of loss. When she saw that even the stump had been dug out, so that there was now no sign that the tree had ever been there, she wept.

Her mother, shocked, had said she hadn't known Tracey was so attached to the tree.

"I just like things to stay the same," said the girl, at which her mother had pursed her lips and nodded seriously, her eyes sad.

They had come to number six Langdale Road a little under a year ago, when Tracey had just turned fifteen, moving from the village eight miles away because her father had got a new job. Jobs were a big deal in the Blenkinsop household, the subject of every dinner time conversation and the brooding silences between them. There weren't enough of them to go round, her mother said, and if her father was 'made redundant' again, they would have to go on the dole. Tracey knew that this meant getting money from the government for not working, which sounded okay to her, but her mother (who worked stacking shelves at Booths) spoke of it with dread and shame.

Somehow Tracey seemed to bear the brunt of all the job-anxiety. Not a day went by when her parents didn't lecture her, singly or together, on the importance of doing well in school, of getting 'qualifications' so that she wouldn't have to worry about work the way they did. Sensing that this was how her parents coped with their precarious professional situations, Tracey just nodded and did her homework as requested, making sure that the first page of every essay, every set of maths problems, was extra neat. That was the bit they looked at before saying she could listen to her records in bed.

There had been nothing unusual about the house until a week ago, the day the workmen had come to look at the pear tree. Tracey had watched them talking to her father, shading their eyes as they gazed up at the old, protecting branches, until one of them – the young one in the denim jacket who winked at her and called her 'missus' – looked up and saw her in the window. She had turned quickly away, not wanting him to think she had been watching him, and her eyes had fallen on a book she had left on her bed.

It was a paperback, little more than a pamphlet, really, which her parents had bought for her to make the move more appealing: *Myths and Legends of Old Preston*. Tracey had seen through her parents' attempt to make the grubby, ordinary little streets feel interesting, and she had never looked at it until that day. She had retreated to her room to get away from the watchful eyes of her mother who wanted to console her for the loss of the tree, and she had picked up the slim little paperback to take her mind off things.

It hadn't worked. The book was full of silliness, stories that ranged from the comically unbelievable to the merely sad. She skimmed only a few pages before putting it aside, deciding to think about something else, then reached for her little cassette player and pressed play. She regularly recorded selections from the Radio 1 Top 40 countdown on Sunday night and was compiling a list of the albums she'd like for Christmas. Her taste was specific but hard to classify. Number one this week was the Police's 'Don't Stand So Close to Me,' which she liked, though she was tiring of it, but she had recently heard new songs by Kate Bush ('Army Dreamers') and a curiously upbeat electronic thing about the first atomic bomb. It was called 'Enola Gay,' but she didn't know the band, and she was hoping to catch it on the radio so she could give it a proper listen. If Kellie Marie's 'Feels Like I'm in Love' came on the radio she would make vomit noises until it finished. Carol Drinkwater (her best friend at school and the owner of the second stupidest name in the history of the world) thought that Roxy Music's 'Over You' was the greatest song ever recorded, but that was just because she fancied Bryan Ferry. He could sing 'Row, Row, Row your Boat' and Carol would say it was the greatest song ever recorded.

Tracey grinned to herself as the music played, and opened her wardrobe to get the tortoiseshell clip for her hair which was getting too long again. She wouldn't admit it to anyone, but she liked her hair. It was the only thing about the way she looked that she did like, but still. It was a rich chestnut colour that turned copper in the right light, and it made her face more interesting than it had any right to be. Especially her eyes, which were a muddy green, and her skin which was pale to the point of pastiness . . .

The wardrobe door had a full length mirror on the inside, and as she opened it she caught her reflection in the glass and gasped. There was a pale boy standing behind her, staring, his mouth moving, his eyes full of rage.

Preston held on as best he could, but the sight of the girl had filled him with so much anger and confusion that he knew his grip on her world, her time, would be momentary at best. He had shouted, demanding who she was and what she was doing in his house, but the light was already fading. Astonishingly, she had seen him. He didn't know how that was possible, but he was sure of it. He had seen the flicker of shock in her eyes, though the response had been fleeting and there was no understanding in her face. There was only outrage which had turned instantly to bewilderment, so that he was sure she had lost him. He was also sure that he had seen her before.

In life.

But only just. He had seen her the night he had died, mere moments before, in fact. She had been on Woodside Avenue with her family who were, he recalled, looking at a house that was for sale, complaining that the kitchen was too small . . .

So they had bought his. He had died, his parents had . . . what? Sold the house. Or was it worse than that? Had they too died? The house had looked so strange. It might have been decades since he died.

Preston fought to scrabble back into the girl's room, but he felt uncertain, thrown by the strangeness of the place, of the time, and her presence in it. He couldn't focus, couldn't hold on, and before she had turned to face him, he was, once more, alone in the dark, the room sliding back to the way he had known it. Preston hung his head, knowing that the comforting familiarity of the place as it was – Spitfires, guitar, bird chart and all – was part of the reason he had failed.

* * *

Tracey blinked. There was, of course, no boy in her room. If there had been, she would have given him a swift kick where it hurt.

But there wasn't. She spun away from the mirror, but the room was empty, and there was no lingering image in the mirror itself when she turned back to it. She had imagined the boy. The hair on her neck was standing on end, her skin felt cold, and her heart was racing, but that was just that chemical stuff that came from your brain, wasn't it? Adrenaline. If you imagined something, your body would respond. It didn't mean that what you thought you'd seen was real.

And what had she seen? A boy, his face almost white, his hair dark – black, she thought – his eyes hooded under long lashes. His lips were thin but sensitive. He might have looked sullen, but he was wearing, she was fairly sure, some kind of uniform, green with some sort of strange neck tie. The thought touched a vague memory, like the soft resonance of a distant bell, but she couldn't recall anything clearly and the more she tried, the more it seemed to slip away from her.

* * *

As soon as his strength returned, Preston left the house and ran up Langdale Road, making for the cemetery. If his parents were dead, he would find them there. He didn't want to but he had to know. Yet, as he reached the top of the street, only yards from where he had died, he stopped suddenly. A sound was drifting down from the corner of Stuart Road. The sound of children singing.

Preston kept very still, straining to hear but listening with a gaunt horror, remembering Roarer's vague, scared warnings. He knew the song vaguely. It was old, the kind of song that you got taught in infant school, the kind whose tune got put to various school yard limericks and obscenities. But whoever was singing this was doing what Preston took to be the original. It echoed, fading in and out like it was transmitting over a bad telephone line, but he could still make out the words.

"Early one morning
Just as the sun was rising
I heard a maiden singing
In the valley below.
Oh, don't deceive me.
Oh, never leave me.
How could you use a poor maiden so?"

Why the song made him so uneasy, Preston couldn't say, but there was something about those haunting, unsteady voices, something soulless in the sound. The point was driven home as, that one verse and chorus completed, they began again without so much as a pause. And now he could see them, a tight group of a dozen or so kids, his age or less, shambling together and singing their endless looping song, their eyes empty.

Preston didn't even consider trying to speak to them.

These were the kids Roarer had spoken of with dread, and Preston knew instinctively they were not what they seemed. They came stumbling on, an ungainly huddle as if they were bound together by some invisible rope, raggedly cooing out their awkward song (*"Oh, don't deceive me. Oh, never leave me . . ."*), their eyes blank. They were getting closer, and as they did so, they all raised their right arms out in front of them, their tiny fingers reaching . . .

Preston stepped quickly backwards, then turned and began retracing his steps, breaking into a steady run that took him past number six and all the way down to Cromwell Road. He would go to the cemetery the long way. At the corner he risked a look back, though he knew the eerie singing had already faded.

The huddle of children hadn't pursued him.

The relief he felt was immeasurable and baffling. It was after all, just a song, just more ghosts like him, trapped in some awful, obsessive loop like the Brakeman. It shouldn't be this unsettling.

But it was.

At the top of Cromwell Road, Preston turned left onto Ribbleton Avenue, crossing the street so he would be as far from Stuart Road as possible, and he walked carefully now, so that he would hear the ghostly singing if it was close by. He glanced around constantly, but there was no sign of the spectral children, and he reached the cemetery gates without incident. After his almost-encounter with the children the graveyard held no terror for him, and he was unsurprised to see no signs of ghostly activity there. This was, after all, merely the place they put your bones. It wasn't where the dead had lived, and it was only the fact that he had been there as an altar boy that meant he could get in at all.

Preston knew that he didn't have the skill or energy to

materialise in the world of the living and wander for ages before returning to his own time, so he had to try to figure out where the newest graves would be. He was searching for his parents, but he did not know how much time had passed since his death and had no good reason to think his parents had also died except that someone else lived in his house now, someone he had seen the very night he died.

Nice uniform.

The girl with the chestnut hair and frank, appraising eyes. In his damned room. Was it merely coincidence that the last person he had seen alive now lived in his house? And if she looked now largely as she had on the night he died, then his sense that decades might have passed was surely wrong. More likely his parents had moved away shortly after his death. The house would have been too big, too aggressively empty without him. He could almost hear his parents saying it and his grief made him angry at the people who had taken up residence there. Her in particular. She hadn't been scared of him so much as annoyed that he had appeared without permission. It was his bloody room and she was angry at his showing up? Maybe he'd haunt her until she fled, screaming. That would show her.

But if only a little time had passed since he died, then it was less likely that his parents were also dead, not unless something awful had happened . . .

Preston was as sure as he could be that his parents would never commit suicide, no matter how terrible their grief, but he pushed the idea away with difficulty, feeling a new and worrying threat of guilt. He tried to focus. Searching the cemetery in the living present would take hours, while all he could manage at the moment was a couple of seconds. The last thing he wanted was to think that if they were indeed there, he was directly responsible. The thought cluttered his mind, making him angry.

And what he would do if he found his parents' graves, he didn't know. Say goodbye? Say he was sorry? No. It wasn't like he had left them, he thought, his irritation spiking. Not by choice. *They* were the ones who had moved away before he could reach them. *They* were the ones who had made him go to Scouts, which was why he had died in the first place. *They* were too busy objecting to that 'disreputable' leather jacket, as if his father was the mayor and it would reflect badly on him if his son showed an ounce of personality, of rebellion. It was so petty. So ordinary. So like them.

He felt his anger rising. It felt good, safer and more powerful than guilt or grief, so he held onto it, even though a part of him knew it was nonsense.

The old days when graves had been reused were long gone, so that meant the cemetery would expand until it was full. Preston knew it stretched all the way across Miller Road to New Hall Lane, where the oldest graves were, and which went down to the motorway and the Tickled Trout. As a kid he had gone looking for the grave of George Smith, padre to the British forces at the battle of Rorke's Drift which they'd put in that *Zulu* film. The new graves – the ones he had stood beside as an altar boy – were closer to the gates on Ribbleton Avenue. He opted to walk along the funeral route he remembered until he reached the barrier that marked the end of his experience in life. He would try to move into the present – whenever that was – from there.

As he walked, he thought about standing in his black cassock and white cotta, holding the tall brass-topped crucifix beside a dozen graves. He remembered the smell of the incense and the tears of the grieving. He had always felt sorry for them, the families in black, but he had also felt separate, like he was intruding on something private. He had avoided their eyes, and on the occasion that one of them pressed a few coins into his hand, he had been embarrassed and uncomfortable. He had contrived to trade the money with a kid at school so that, in the strictest sense, he never actually spent it. What could you buy with the money someone gave you for helping out at a funeral? All that old love and loss traded for Mars bars and records?

Preston passed the darkened headstones with their

occasional statues of angels and saints, trying – as he had always done – to find the oldest that were still legible. Some of the newer ones, instead of grass on top, were covered with the bright green crystalline stones which Gez Simpson had said were part of the Bannister Doll ritual. You waited until midnight and then rapped on the banister rail three times, saying the name of the ghost each time. The spirit, he said, would come, but you would only see it if you had one of those little green stones from the graveyard.

Preston shuddered at the thought. He hadn't believed the story. Not really. It had frightened him in that fleeting way that the late night horror films frightened him: a brief, permitted fear of what he knew wasn't real. But now he knew the stories *were* true, or at least some of them, and since the very last thing he wanted to see again was the Bannister Doll, he moved quickly away from the nearest grave and its glassy green stones.

The central avenue which had been lined with tall, dark trees at the approach from the main gates opened wide and there were junctions, access roads radiating out in straight lines to other parts of the cemetery like the carefully laid out grid of a housing development. Preston kept going straight until he was close to the Victorian graves beyond the crossing at Miller Road, then he cut left. Almost immediately, the air seemed to harden in front of him.

In life he had not been past this point and it was closed to him now. Ahead was roughly tended grass – more meadow than lawn – and no headstones. This would be the place. In whatever future had already happened for the living there would be new graves in this spot.

He closed his eyes and thought hard, picturing a family grave with his own name on it, fighting down the surge of emotion such an image produced as he clung to the need to simply see it. He imagined daylight on the path he could not now walk, and when he heard the harsh, flat caw of a rook, he opened his eyes.

The image was shifting, but it was there, a row of headstones in bleak, pale sunlight and an overcast sky. Some of the graves were clearly new, polished black granite with gold etched lettering. He took a tentative step and was elated to find that he was both in the world of the living and in a place he had never been in life. He turned to the nearest headstone and read aloud.

"Here lies Agnes Fitzpatrick, beloved wife to Arthur and mother to Lyn, Samuel and David, taken from this life 14th March, 1980."

Preston gasped.

He knew time had passed in ways he had not perceived, but *two years*? And though the grave looked new it might not be the most recent. Just how long had he been dead?

He took a few quick steps, looked wildly about, spotted another recent looking monument – this one grander than the last and with a pale stone Virgin at the grave head, and scanned for a date.

"1979," he read, relieved that it was no later.

Two years though . . .

He hesitated, overcome by the truth of the thing, realising he would never find his parents' graves in the time he had, even if they were there to find, and with that realisation the light around him flickered and went dark. As the colours drained to nothing, Preston turned and started hurrying back to where he had crossed over, but his sudden anxiety sapped his strength. Before he knew it, the world was gone, and with a new horror Preston realised that he was not back in the night of his death . . .

Nine twenty-two.

He hadn't made it the crucial few yards to where he had moved into the present. He had strayed from the world he had known in life, and now there was nothing but blackness around him. There were no trees, no graves, nothing to tell him where he was. He was stranded between worlds.

* * *

Tracey spent a long time standing at the mirror over the

next few hours, turning suddenly and glancing out of the corner of her eye, almost daring the boy she had seen – or thought she had seen – to reappear.

He didn't.

But while this would have convinced some girls that she had merely imagined the whole thing, Tracey – who was not remotely fanciful, was, in fact, frequently accused by her father of being relentlessly logical and able to argue the hind leg off a donkey – would not let the matter go. She considered the way the light bounced from the mirror as if correcting the angle would reveal some ordinary explanation for what she had seen, even checking the back of the wardrobe for camera equipment or projectors, though she could think of no one who would either want to target her or be capable of such a sophisticated practical joke. And as she teased at the possibilities, the memory of what she had seen – not imagined, *seen* – continued to nag at her. She thought of the boy's face, its pallor, its dark, hollow eyes and the slight graze on his cheek. And then there was the uniform. How would her mind have conjured up something so specific, so detailed?

Quietly, as if to squeeze the idea past her meticulously rational mind before it noticed, she allowed herself to acknowledge the possibility that the boy had been both real and inexplicable according to the terms of conventional science. She then asked what such a thing meant. Was she going crazy, seeing things that weren't there like Katie Clarkson's mother who was always in the hospital?

Yet in spite of all this, her dominant feeling was still one of anger. How dare he – whatever he was – come into her room? And if he was real, how many times before had he been there without her knowledge, prying through her things, watching her as she did her homework, or slept or – she thought with a flash of furious embarrassment – got dressed?

If she ever saw the ghost again, he would get an earful for starters.

The ghost.

She frowned at the word, doubting it. But then she picked up the little *Myths and Legends* book and started to read.

CHAPTER 4

Preston took a breath to steady himself and turned very slowly on the spot. Around him was nothing but darkness but if he could perhaps retrace his steps, he might find his way back into his own reality. If there was a similar barrier on this side, of course, then he might be trapped in this lightless nothing forever, but there was no point dwelling on that. He swallowed, and tried to remember which way he had been facing before he turned.

The graves had both been on his right. He made a quarter turn to his left and tried to recall how far he had walked before that. Five yards? Ten? Not much more, surely. He stared into the blackness ahead trying to remember everything he had done. If he walked in the wrong direction, each attempt to correct might take him further and further away from where he needed to be so that he might never find the way out.

Assuming there was one . . .

He swallowed that thought down. There must be a route back. He just had to find it.

He took three careful steps forward, his arms outstretched for any sign of the invisible barrier. Nothing. He took three more, paused and then another two. He should have found it by now. He was starting to panic. He turned a half circle and counted out the eight steps that should put him back where he had started. Perhaps his sense of direction had been off. He clenched his teeth, fighting back the urge to sob, and tried to decide which way to go. With nothing to focus on, it was impossible, like playing Blind Man's Buff after you've been spun around. He rotated another fraction to his left.

He took ten careful strides in the blackness, then stopped, turned just as carefully, and returned to where he had been. He might have been crying now if his eyes could still produce tears, and as the desperation mounted, he became steadily more muddled so that he could not be sure which directions he had already tried. He repeated the whole process, increasingly sure that there was no way back, then stopped, turned a little more and tried again. He took five, eight, ten paces and there was still nothing. He hesitated, then took two more. Still nothing. In desperation, he added another, but there was no lessening of the darkness around him. He reached vaguely ahead, forcing down the impulse to just run screaming in circles, and felt a curious thickening of the air. He stopped, pushed his hands out further and leaned against the yielding barrier he could not see. His balance tugged him forward and, almost against his will, he took one more step.

And suddenly, he was through.

He was back in the cemetery. It was night. It was nine twenty-two on 15th September, 1978, or his version of that moment, and miserable though that fact had come to make him, it now brought only relief. For better or worse, he was home. His body felt the same as ever but there was a grey weariness in his mind that felt like age, so that it took a moment to realise that dimly, on the edge of his hearing he could make out the baying of a pack of dogs pounding through the church yard, getting closer.

Before he had even fixed the direction of the sound, Preston began to run.

* * *

Mrs. Nora Macintyre stood up straight with difficulty, one hand on her back, the other clutching the dead flowers she had removed from the grave. It wasn't her job, cleaning up the cemetery, she thought. She had enough on her hands with the church. All that brass to polish, flowers to arrange, altar cloths and vestments to mend and launder, all invariably spotted with candle wax at that. It wasn't like anyone showed any real appreciation, though Father Edwards would be quick to complain if she let up for a minute.

She frowned, shaking the dead stalks until the petals fell like brown feathers among the headstones, and turned, vaguely aware of someone close by, someone who had approached in total silence as she worked. You got strange types in the cemetery these days, winos and homeless people sheltering among the graves, and there was talk of drug deals and Lord knew what else taking place in the darkness of the trees. She was immediately on her guard.

But the figure she had seen was only a skinny boy, fourteen or fifteen years old, and wearing a green uniform. Maybe a school uniform. But it wasn't quite green. In fact, as she looked, she realised there was something curiously insubstantial about it, a vague translucent quality. He moved and she could see the great steepling cross of the Jenkins grave right through his shirt.

Mrs. Macintyre kept very still, her breath held, and a half-prayer rose to her lips, but before the words could form themselves the boy turned, unseeing, towards her, and she gasped. He was only there for a moment before fading entirely to nothing, but she saw the face clearly, and with a stifled sob that brought one hand to her heart, she spoke the dead boy's name aloud.

"Preston Oldcorn."

* * *

Preston sprinted away from the sound of the pack, back the way he had come, along the paths that wound through the graves, then onto the tree-lined road to the cemetery gates and out onto Ribbleton Avenue. He glanced behind him only once, glimpsing a seething mass in the distant gloom behind him. Without the sound of their barking he would not have even known for sure they were dogs. But they were in pursuit, and with a shock of horror Preston realised that since the ghost hounds were like him, they would not tire.

He accelerated toward town, driven by the memory of Roarer's ravaged hand, passed Woodlands Avenue, to Blackpool Road and on, under the brittle and ineffective glow of the blue-white street lamps. He passed the dirty brick walls of houses, shops and pubs near the top of Acregate Lane at a flat run. There was no stitch in his chest, no laboured breathing, no screaming muscles but he felt something akin to exhaustion swelling in his mind like he was dragging a great weight behind him.

Part of that weight was worry: he didn't get tired, but no body – alive or dead – was built to sustain this pace over this distance. He had already covered at least a mile and a half at the speed he would have reserved for a forty yard dash. What if he wore out some crucial piece of cartilage, broke a tiny, but vital bone, or strained a ligament to breaking? He would not heal, and the dogs wouldn't give him the chance. Because that was the other part of the worry smouldering in his mind: they were getting closer.

As he passed Skeffington Road, he risked a look over his shoulder. They were a boiling wave of flailing paws and arching backs. There were at least a dozen of them, maybe more, a few small and muttish, others like Alsatians and Dobermans, with one that was bigger still, a Wolfhound the size of a small pony. They were wild, mad-eyed, driven by the blind yearning of a thirst they could not slake, and all their attention was focused on Preston. They would not turn aside or fall squabbling among themselves. They had one mind between them and it dreamed only of tearing his fragile body.

So he ran on, along Ribbleton Lane, past the Victorian chimneys of Horrocks' mill, past the high walls of the old prison, all the while shoving his anxieties into the darkest part of his mind, fighting to get hold of a strategy.

Why hadn't he asked Roarer how he had escaped with the loss of only a couple of fingers? That now seemed like a victory, and one Preston couldn't see himself repeating. They would run him down. They would catch him. They would rip him into joints and then – somehow much worse – they would leave him conscious forever.

He crossed the Ring Way and ran on past The Lamb pub on Church Street, ignoring the turn off to the bus station, and the flag market, keeping straight on past the sculpted elegance of Miller Arcade to the broad windowed shops of Fishergate. Preston pounded the ground beneath him, waiting for the painless twinge, the collapse of a knee or the turn of an ankle that would mean disaster, but in his conscious mind he held a half-idea.

The river.

Roarer had said something about losing the dogs down by the river. Preston didn't know what that meant, whether the scent of the water would confuse them or if he had to swim across, but it was the closest thing to a plan he had. The Ribble ran from the northeast of town, beyond Grimsargh and Ribchester where the old Roman fort had been, down towards the sea at Lytham. If he'd thought of it, he could have cut directly down to where the M6 ran beyond the cemetery, but he didn't know that area well and it was too late now anyway. In town, he thought, as he made a hard left into Winckley Square, the closest point to the water was Avenham Park.

The baying of the hounds was reaching fever pitch. Preston peered round a corner and was horrified to see that they were only a hundred yards behind him now. He could see their mad eyes, their lolling jaws. It wouldn't be long now.

He ran into the gloomy park, down its paths and lawns, under its black trees, and up to the old tramway bridge over the broad, flat river, and they came on behind him without hesitation. He crossed the bridge at the same hard run but the dogs came after him, so that Preston was struck by a sudden despair. Because there was, there could be, no escape. They were relentless, burning to dismember even if they could not eat, and at last Preston slowed, his eyes flashing around for something, *anything*, that might provide help or distraction.

And he saw it: a block of men in curious clothes, marching together, twenty or more of them on the river bank.

Preston's eyes widened and he picked up speed again, making for them and shouting for help as he did so. As he got close, however, he saw the lamp light sparkle on what he thought were hats . . .

Helmets, in fact. They wore armour of a bright grey metal, laced together over crimson tunics. They bore large rectangular shields which curved slightly to fit their bodies, wore short swords at their waists, and shouldered spears with long and dangerous-looking tips. Cloaks were pulled around them and one, the officer, had a helmet crested with a red plume.

Roman legionaries!

Preston, who had been fascinated with them as a kid, would have known them anywhere.

For a second the strange delight of it doused all other thoughts, and when he came to himself again the dogs were almost on him. He cried out in panic, and the legionaries, reacted, whirling towards him, angling their shields before their chests, and reversing the grips on their spears so that they pointed directly, lethally at him.

"No!" Preston shouted. "I'm not your enemy! They are!"

He waved wildly at the hounds which streamed over the bridge, baying their mad hunger, and though the soldiers' eyes were doubtful, they fixed on the dogs and their resolve stiffened. The officer growled *"Barbaros interficio!"* and suddenly they had all taken up the words so they became a chant, as the soldiers locked together in formation. Preston peeled off, trying to get out from between the two foes, but the officer drew his sword and before Preston could say another word, the battle started.

The appearance of other people was probably the only thing that would have made the dogs forget him. Now faced not with one stringy boy but a company of men whose muscle was taut and plentiful, the hounds' eyes grew wide and greedy. They hurled themselves at the patrol without thought for their own safety, and for a moment the roar of barking was replaced by the thud of their bodies against the Roman shields. Then came the snapping of jaws, the hiss of penetrating steel, the tearing of clothes, fur and flesh. Though there was no blood, no pain, Preston looked away.

He turned back to the fight at a shout of panic from the men. The wolfhound had charged the shield wall like a rhino, dipping under the spear points and hitting the soldiers so hard that their defences buckled. Two men fell and the huge dog burst through, snapping, three Alsatians in pursuit. One of them took a spear lunge clean through its hind quarters but the dog barely broke stride. One man went down and the Doberman dragged him clear. As another of the Romans fought to reach his stricken comrade, the massive wolfhound pounced, its yellow knife-like fangs slicing. Another man went down. But then one of the legionaries dropped his spear and cut at the beast's legs with his sword. The monstrous dog winced away, wary, and as the other soldiers switched to their swords, the tide turned.

There was something curiously mechanical about the way the Romans fought, the way they stood and stared. They were reacting to the dogs, but they seemed as if they were fighting in their sleep, barely aware of what was happening. The ghost dogs were only minimally slowed by the stab wounds inflicted by the slender spears, but none of them could afford to lose a paw to those keen sword blades. The wolfhound dodged once, twice, then skittered back out of range. The Alsatians joined the retreat and — all of a sudden — it was over.

In moments the dogs had scattered yelping and limping into the night. The wounded Romans re-joined their brother soldiers. One had pale flesh hanging from the bones of his left arm, his face scarred by paws and fangs, but he was still walking.

"I'm sorry," said Preston. "I didn't know you would be here. I'm glad you were, of course, but . . ."

The officer's hard face did not alter, nor did he lower the sword aimed at Preston's throat. For a moment there was only the receding howls of the dog pack, and then the officer — his eyes vague, as if he wasn't really seeing Preston at all — spoke, a short and guttural sentence which might have been a question or a command, uttered in a language Preston did not know.

"Oh," Preston said, uneasy. "You speak Latin, don't you? We use that in church sometimes, but I don't really understand it."

The officer continued to look at him the way the Brakeman did, as if he wasn't really seeing him, but then he turned his face down as if he was looking at Preston's feet. As he did so, Preston realised that though he was not a particularly tall boy, his eyes were almost level with the soldier's, and for the first time he noted a curious detail he had missed in the frenzy of the battle. Every soldier seemed sunk into the ground to their mid-calf, their feet completely invisible.

"Why . . . ?" he began, but caught himself, partly because he knew they would not understand, partly because as he was looking at their feet, they were gazing uncertainly at his. Suddenly they were all voicing that same Latin phrase over and over – *Barbaros interficio* – and as they did so they seemed to come to some kind of group verdict and, moving as one, they trained their weapons on Preston.

He thought fast, trying to recall what little he knew about the town's Roman heritage. He had visited the excavations at Ribchester, ten miles or so upstream, where there had been a fort and a villa, where a famous bronze cavalry helmet had been found. The Romans had been able to ford the river there, he remembered. There had been the remains of one of those rooms they always showed in the history books, the ones with the stone floor supports under which they drove the hot air to warm the building. Ribchester was probably where the soldiers had been going when they were attacked close to two thousand years ago.

But the Roman ground level was lower than the present,

wasn't it? You had to dig a couple of feet down to where the Roman roads had been.

"You are walking on the ground as you knew it," he said aloud, gazing down to where the officer's feet should have been. "Which means . . . that to your eyes, I'm floating in the air. So were the dogs!"

"Barbaros interficio!"

That couldn't be good. If they were still capable of thought, they'd assume he was some kind of spirit or demon, that he had brought the hounds with him. And if they were to march him up to Ribchester instead of slaughtering him on the spot, he was going to have a serious problem. He had been to ruins before, but always by car on the modern roads which ran up through Grimsargh. If they were to lead him along the east bank of the river he would quickly hit the barrier that marked the limits of where he had been in life. If they couldn't take him with them he doubted they would simply set him free to attack some other time with his hoard of floating demon dogs . . . But one look at their nebulous expressions and he knew he was overthinking the situation. They had been dead a long time. They had their own version of the madness which drove the dogs, the obsessive repetition which so compelled the Brakeman. They were just conscious enough to recognise that he was not one of them, and now other ancient instincts would kick in. They would kill him, or give it their very best shot.

The phrase they were chanting over and over grew louder.

"Barbaros interficio!"

Kill the barbarian? He'd bet his life – if he had one – on it. The dogs, Preston, anything that wasn't a Roman soldier on their endless patrol was a barbarian to be destroyed. He looked hastily around him, hoping the dogs might still provide a diversion, but they had gone back over the bridge and disappeared.

The bridge . . .

The bridge had iron sides. It had been built for trams . . .

Preston twisted out of the grasp of the soldier behind him and, his hands still bound in the small of his back, dashed back the way he had come. The legionaries came after him, as he knew they would, but as he mounted the path up to the bridge, they faltered. One of them flung his spear and as Preston ducked he saw it pass through what to him was the solid wall of the bridge, and vanish. The tramway was no more than a hundred and fifty years old. To the Romans, who would have had to walk all the way up to Ribchester to cross the river, it was a bridge of the future, something they wouldn't be able to see, and certainly couldn't use.

So Preston ran, and as he moved out across the bridge

they couldn't see, their chant slackened off and their eyes grew vague again. On the other side of the water he stopped and turned back, watching as they forgot him completely, returning to their slow march along the opposite bank.

There was no sign of the dogs. Exulted, Preston put one hand to his chest and had to remind himself that he would find no heartbeat. He was as much a ghost as the soldiers and the dogs. How long it would be before he became mindless like them, trapped in some ancient and constricted sense of what life had been, he could not say. He feared it would not take long.

CHAPTER 5

Nora Macintyre knelt at the back of the empty church lost
in thought. The Church of the Blessed Sacrament was a
great brick, vertical barn of a building, built for capacity
rather than mood, and when it was deserted as it was now
it felt like a shell, as if something that should be living
inside it was missing or dead. In truth, this was how she
liked it, lonely though it was, just her and the stillness of
the sanctuary, even the great too-life-like crucifix and the
tabernacle were distant and somehow abstract. Up close
she'd worry about the polish on the altar rail, the wilt of
the flowers, but back here it was just a dimly lit space, like
a hangar or a cave, and it suited her thoughts.

You couldn't be a priest's housekeeper, she had long
since decided, without deep religious conviction, but
you also couldn't be a priest's housekeeper without those

convictions being tested, strained and refashioned. Sometimes the things she believed and the things she didn't seemed to have shifted so much over the years she was no longer clear she really was a Catholic at all, a thought which would have once worried her a great deal. Not so much now, which was, she supposed, a case in point. She might fail to meet the standards of canon law or papal doctrine, but her faith was bigger and more adaptable than either, and if either she or the Church's lawmakers and teachers were in the wrong she had grown used to the idea that it was probably them, not her.

She hoped the thought wasn't blasphemous, but doubted she could abandon it even if it was.

She had come to think about the boy she had seen in the cemetery: Preston Oldcorn. He had been gone, she thought, about two years now. She had known him, though not well, because he had been an altar boy. He was a quiet, gangly kid, probably bright, if a little broody, the kind of boy who probably went to church to please his parents but would – unless he could find a version of her own theological flexibility – stop soon.

He had died suddenly, she recalled. Collapsed on his way home from the local Scout meeting. Some sort of heart condition, she thought, something no one had diagnosed before, made fatal by shock or exertion. Perhaps he had been running and had overdone it. There had been whisperings amongst some of the other altar boys that he had been restless, unhappy, but there had been no hint of him being suicidal and the police report had found no trace of drugs in his system.

She didn't remember all the details and they had never, she thought, been entirely satisfactory anyway. The effect his death had on his parents had been nothing short of crippling. She had seen them at the funeral. *Devastated,* was the word. It had never seemed so completely right to her. Their faces were like one of those photographs of a blasted landscape from the First World War, the trees sheared off a few feet above the ground and nothing growing in the acres of cratered mud.

It had been hard on her, she remembered, a replaying of her baby brother's death when she was young. It brought back all those old feelings, watching her parents slipping away from her and the world as they collapsed into their grief. Barry would have been a year or two older than Preston Oldcorn when he died. She hadn't thought of him much over the last decade or so, but now she could see his face as fresh and clear as if she was looking at a photograph. She imagined the agony of seeing him again as some half-translucent wraith flitting between the grave stones, like the shadow she had glimpsed of the boy that had been Preston

Oldcorn, and tears started to form in her eyes. It was hard enough to lose a brother or a son. Nobody should have to see them in that spectral form, because that dashed to pieces even the hope that they were at least at peace.

He wasn't the first ghost Nora Macintyre had seen, though it had been a long time since she had glimpsed a shape she knew no one else could see, and she kept such things to herself always. They made her uneasy in her soul, guilty, as if her occasional ability to spy into death was a sin. This time, however, she felt something different, something still more unsettling. Something like anger.

She stared up at the crucifix, dimly aware that she had strayed from the woolly middle ground between thought and prayer which was her usual mental state in church. She was not talking to God at all. She was talking to herself, and that itself was an act which, for Nora Macintyre, was touched with defiance.

No, Preston Oldcorn was not the first ghost she had seen but he was, in his youth and familiarity, the saddest, the most dreadful. If his parents were to hear of it . . . That was too awful to consider. She didn't know what it meant that she had seen him, and privately hoped it would never happen again, but if he returned, if he showed himself once more to her or others, she would have to do something. What, she had no idea. But something.

* * *

Roarer thought Preston's running from the dogs all the way from the cemetery to the river was hilarious.

"But that's what *you* did!" Preston protested.

"Not from here," said Roarer, gesturing around the graveyard wildly. "I was already in town when they spotted me, wasn't I? Quick run down through the park and there it was: the river. I didn't have to run a marathon. You legged it all the way from here? Why didn't you just go inside somewhere and close the door?"

He laughed some more, then started acting the event out, shrieking as he glanced over his shoulder "Ooh, the dogs are coming! The dogs are coming. I'd better hike to, like, *Manchester* to get away from them!"

"At least I kept all my fingers," Preston snapped back through his own grin. Roarer's laughter was always infectious.

"This is true," Roarer confessed, glancing sourly at his own hand. "Still, not sure I would have run all the way through town to save them. Too much like hard work."

"It's not like we get tired," Preston said, squatting on a mouldering tomb and crossing his legs.

"Too bad we can't run in the Olympics," said Roarer. "Can you imagine? We'd blow right by every record there was. Pow. Just like that." He made a sudden movement with his good hand, like he was throwing a dart. "We should try."

"Set up our own competition, you mean?"

"No, I mean go to the actual Olympics and race on the same track with the runners."

"How would we do that?" asked Preston.

"Some ghosts, I've heard," said Roarer, gazing up at the unchanging night sky, "when they are really old and strong like we will be one day, they can move not just into the living present, but into any moment between that and when they were alive. We could go to London for the 1948 Olympics. Run right by Tom Richards and that Argentine bloke. Course, I wasn't actually there, so I couldn't go back even if I knew how to . . ."

Preston sat up.

"We can go back to when we were alive?" he said. "What, and just watch, or actually get into that time so that people there could see us?"

"Maybe," Roarer shrugged. "It's hard though. I've never known a ghost that could actually do it. Except . . ."

He faltered and rolled onto his stomach.

"What?" said Preston. "Which ghost could do it?"

"You know," said Roarer. "The one that looks like kids but isn't."

"The Doll?"

"I don't know," said Roarer, his good humour gone. "Maybe. It's just what I heard."

"But if we could go back in time, step into our own lives," Preston persisted, "maybe we could do something, say something to someone or even to our living selves, that would stop us from getting killed."

Roarer peered at him from the gloom, his face screwed up with scepticism.

"I don't see how that could work," he said. "And like I said. It's too hard."

"We have to learn how to do it," said Preston, all earnestness now. "I could go back to the day I died and – I don't know – not go to Scouts that night. Something. I could change the past and then I wouldn't die."

"Then it would just get you another time," said Roarer, who had grown suddenly sullen.

"Why?" said Preston. "Might not. Then I'd be alive and not stuck here."

Roarer's scowl deepened.

"Even if I couldn't save myself I'd get to see different places and people," Preston went on. "Like watching history as it happened around me. That would be cool. Make a change from this at least."

"You're no fun anymore," Roarer said, looking away.

"I don't mean I hate it here," said Preston quickly. "But being alive again. That would be great, wouldn't it?"

Roarer just shrugged again, his back to him.

"Going for a walk," he muttered, getting to his feet and then hesitating a half second, as if waiting for Preston to call him back. When he didn't, Roarer scowled, then walked sullenly away.

Preston watched him shuffle off, his shoulders sloped, but he couldn't feel his friend's despondency. If there was a way into the living past as well as the present, then this endless nowhere night could be changed.

* * *

It had been a week since Tracey Blenkinsop had seen the ghost boy. She hadn't told anybody because she wanted to be sure in her own head that it had been real before she risked making a fool of herself to someone else. She wanted to decide who that someone else would be carefully, not just blurting it out because the idea of being haunted made her feel alone. If she told her mother she would get concern, worry which would infect the family and make them watchful of her. If she told her dad, she'd get common-sense logic and, if she didn't shrug it off quickly, irritation touched with disappointment. Both parents would tell each other right away, so the moment all three of them were together they'd have one of those talks where it felt like the air had grown heavy and would stay that way until she laughed and said it was nothing, that everything was fine. Then they'd have tea, and maybe they'd play Monopoly and her dad would lecture her on why she couldn't expect to win with nothing but the railway stations because you had to build . . .

That was how Tracey's family handled crisis: talk, tea, and Monopoly.

Of course, she could tell Carol Drinkwater, who would gasp and put her hands to the sides of her face like a cartoon character before wondering why *she* didn't get to see a ghost, and pronouncing that Tracey was *so* lucky, even if it was horrible and scary . . .

But Tracey needed to be sure first, and that meant seeing the ghost again. She spent as much time as possible up in her room, one eye on the mirror as she pored over the *Myths and Legends* book, but nothing happened. Once when she had been sitting up there, staring out into the street past where the pear tree had stood, she caught a flash of light in the mirror, but it was just the headlamps of a car pulling out of number three. She frowned at it, wondering briefly if her ghost boy had been no more than that, a trick of the light.

No. She knew what she had seen, even if she never saw it again.

She read the *Myths and Legends* book cover to cover several times. It was full of stories of odd happenings in the area, some of them so absurd that they were actually funny – like the Longridge boggart which threw its head at people – and some just grim little snatches of history – children struck by passing trains, a girl beaten to death by her own father. That was the only one that bothered her, and her unease was less about the tales of the girl's ghost than it was about the manner of her death. Tracey might not have a particularly strong imagination but her greatest gift, her mother had once said, was her ability to empathise with others. At the time, Tracey had needed to look the word up, marvelling that something could suit her so perfectly. *A gift for understanding the way other people felt*, the dictionary said, *for putting yourself in their position and seeing the world as they might*. Tracey, who assumed everyone did this, decided it was a good thing, and took pride in sharing her mother's observation with whomever would listen, until her mother told her that if she was really sensitive to other people's feelings she would shut up about it. As she had gotten older, she had learned to keep her empathy more tightly leashed. Giving it full rein seemed a pretty good way of getting hurt, especially where boys were concerned.

She wondered if empathy had something to do with her sighting of the ghost boy, that it somehow made her sensitive to his presence, but she doubted it. She felt no connection to the ghost. Just irritation at his barging into her room, her life, as if he belonged there.

Still, the idea that she might have some kind of gift that made her sensitive to the presence of spirits or souls or whatever they were appealed to her, even if it was a bit creepy. Tracey liked the idea of secret connections with people, and of being deeper, more complex than people assumed. She wanted to be a little mysterious, because she wanted to keep something entirely to herself, a sliver of her soul that was unknowable to the rest of the world. She felt she would have to tell someone about the ghost boy eventually, because that would make it real, but a part of her wanted to keep it stowed away so that no one would ever know.

Unless, of course, the ghost was dangerous. The *Myths and Legends* book was full of horror stories of what the dead did to the living, and she found herself wondering why the boy had sought her out and whether she ought to be afraid as well as angry. She didn't think so. The ghost had looked gloomy, and though his dark eyes had flashed with something like her own fury, she had sensed no malice. Still, maybe she should be on her guard. She considered the book again, then gave her reflection in the wardrobe mirror a long, serious look. She didn't believe he was dangerous, she admitted. And if she was entirely honest with herself, she actually wanted him to come back, just so she would know he had been real, so she could tell him what she thought of him for invading her home, before doing whatever she could to bar him from ever returning.

* * *

Preston spoke to the old Brakeman twice, each time hoping for something new, some shift in his routine that would offer new information to work with. But the Brakeman reacted to him vaguely, so that Preston was not even sure that he remembered meeting him before. At first, the Brakeman offered no more than his usual catalogue of duties, and for Preston, the lack of progress was a mirror of his entire existence: a permanent stasis, a state of being whose temporal limits (nine twenty-two) might as well be the walls of a prison. He scowled at the shadowy figure with his lantern, moving mindlessly through his litany of tasks, knowing he had to find a way out, a way forward, before he got trapped in his own version of the Brakeman's dementia.

"Why does it matter so much to you?" Preston asked. "I mean, there's no train, and even if there was you couldn't do anything about it. If Roarer's right and you can move on to the next world, why don't you do that?"

"Check the brakes on't wagons, check that the points are set, check the wagon loads are stable," said the Brakeman.

"It's because your job got you killed, isn't it?" said Preston. "Or because you didn't do your job properly, right? Or is it because someone else got killed?"

The Brakeman seemed to hesitate at that and his eyes grew vague. Then a curious change came over him, he became rigid, legs splayed, as if fighting for balance on something that was moving. He climbed over a barrier of some sort which Preston couldn't see, and grasped some invisible object in his gnarled hands. There was nothing there, but he held on like the most convincing mime in the world, leaning on it until his face strained with the effort. It looked like he was trying to pull a huge lever. His breath came in great, laboured gasps, but he made no headway and finally abandoned whatever he was doing with a curse.

Preston gaped. The Brakeman was reliving his own past. For all Preston knew, he was truly in it, able to change what happened that day if he could just escape the pattern he had been reliving ever since . . .

The Brakeman was moving, gingerly picking his way along the line, swaying to keep his balance as if he was hurtling along on the footplate of a train or in an open-topped wagon. Then he was leaning out, muttering under his breath, "Can't reach . . . Can't reach. If I could just . . . reach . . ." His eyes widened in horror, and he flung his hands up in front of his face . . .

And then it, whatever it had been, was over. The Brakeman stood up quite normally, all the desperation and effort draining from his face and body. His eyes got that vague look again, and he returned to his usual pottering.

"Check the brakes on't wagons, check that the points are set, check the wagon loads are stable," he said.

"What was that?" asked Preston. "What you just did. Was that how you died? Something jammed, or broke and you couldn't fix it. Is that it? Couldn't you do something different this time?"

"Check the brakes on't wagons . . ."

"No," said Preston, "listen. You know you're dead. You remember it. So why do you keep trying to undo it all?"

The Brakeman ignored him, and as he wandered down the line, Preston heard the catalogue mumbled back to him through the gloom. He watched the Brakeman traipsing back and forth in the cutting, and he found himself marvelling at the difference of their predicaments. Unlike the Brakeman, Preston had no obsessive desire to stay, so why hadn't he moved on? Why was he wandering this shell of a town in its perpetual gloom when he could be Sincerely Dead?

He walked back along the line towards town, thinking, and two answers came to him, though they were, perhaps, really the same thing. First, he was scared of what might be waiting if he gave up on his ghostly wandering. It had been easier to believe in an afterlife when his actual life seemed like it would stretch on forever, its end impossibly distant. Now that the reality of the thing was on top of him he felt a cold dread of stepping finally out of the world he had known. He did not fear damnation, for in his heart of hearts he felt sure that he had lived a good life, and had done nothing to incur the wrath of God. But if there was no God after all, no judgment, no anything, that was a different matter entirely. Now that he felt the choice hard and clear in front of him like a junction or one of the Brakeman's railway points, he found his faith was not strong enough. The possibility of leaving this curious Limbo, of stepping into the beyond and simply winking out of existence seemed all too real. This half-life that he had now was surely better than none at all.

And that was the other part of the answer, perhaps the more important part. He just wasn't ready to go yet. He couldn't see his parents here, but he could see his house, his room, and he could imagine them moving through that space, thinking of him, missing him, though he could not perceive them. But maybe one day he would master that too, and not just by glimpsing them for a few exhausting seconds. He had already done that without really trying. Even Roarer had done that. Preston had a gift for it. Maybe one day he would be able to move into the living present effortlessly and stay there as long as he wanted . . .

One day.

Except that it was always the same day, the same night, to be precise, and he was stuck in it. Because the debate about whether or not to move on and join the Sincerely Dead was purely abstract, a mere idea to torment himself with. Whatever he decided would make no difference because he had never been given the option of moving on. There had been no dazzling light into which he could walk, no door, no ladder like the Bible stories had said. He had merely died and woken up in this no place, this lifeless shadow of the world in which he had grown up.

He pushed the display button on his watch and watched the square-sided red numbers flash up. Nine twenty-two. Always.

He had not chosen this. He was merely here.

Preston had no answers to his own situation, but maybe he could still help the Brakeman, and he should focus on that. Instinctively he felt that the key to doing so was in getting a full account of the railway accident that had killed him. Though the Brakeman himself couldn't explain it, there would be other sources. There would be local history books and old newspapers, and Preston knew just where he would be able to get access to them: the Harris Library.

He had been walking along the track passed Gamull Lane and the Cromwell Road bridge, through Deepdale toward the heart of the town, but as he passed under the St Paul's Road bridge, where the railway line ran parallel to Great George Street, he saw something ahead, a dark, swelling blackness like a hole in the night.

The mouth of the Miley Tunnel.

Preston became very still, as if he was listening, but it wasn't hesitation or thought. It wasn't even the memory of what Roarer had said about there being ghosts which could do terrible things to you. Preston could just feel something ahead, a presence in the tunnel, and without needing to think or explore the situation further he knew beyond a shadow of a doubt that he wanted no part of it. There was, to put it mildly, no way he was going to walk into that great black maw, even if he didn't feel the familiar thickening of the air which barred his progress in places he had not been in life.

The tunnel ran about a half mile, give or take, under Lancaster Road, the police station, Moor Lane, St. Peter's

Square, and Adelphi Street, opening up again in Maudland at Cold Bath Street.

The words sent a shudder through Preston's dead bones, as if he were standing in whatever freezing waters had given the place its desolate name.

And then, as if sensing his mood, the singing started. It was the same as before, spectral children's voices curling out of the echoing tunnel like smoke.

> "*Oh, don't deceive me.*
> *Oh, never leave me . . .*"

Preston had never in life or death felt anything like it: it was like a cold stone in his gut that spoke with certainty of unimaginable horrors. For a long moment Preston stood there (*just as the sun was rising, I heard a maiden singing . . .*) and he felt as if the tunnel, or something inside it, was watching him, waiting to see what he would do. At last he was able to tear himself away, shutting the sound of the singing out as he found an embankment he could scramble up. He reached the road, and did not look back.

* * *

Nora Macintyre returned to the cemetery every day, telling

Father Edwards that vandals had made a mess, knocking over flower vases and scrawling PNE and MUFC in marker on some of the headstones. She went with a bucket of supplies and a bottle of rubbing alcohol with rags made, in part, from one of the altar boy's cottas after he had stood too close to an acolyte's candles and done his best to set himself on fire.

Gavin Smithwick. Stupid boy. If brains were chocolate, the whole family together couldn't fill a Smartie.

Not a very charitable thought, she reminded herself, but not wrong for all that.

Cleaning the grave stones, however, was an excuse. She didn't admit it to herself, but she was looking for the Oldcorn boy and didn't know where else to try. The cemetery was where she had seen him, so the cemetery was where she would look.

What she would do if she saw him again, she still didn't know, but she kept an eye out, even as she got down on her aging knees and scrubbed, her mouth set thin and tight, her head full of what she'd say to those young hooligans if she caught them out here with their felt tips and their cans of paint. When she was finished but had still seen nothing out of the ordinary, she made her way over to where her parents and her brother Barry were buried.

The grass had grown long around the graves here. She'd

be getting on to the town council about that. What did she pay her taxes for if they couldn't do something as simple as mow grass? It had rained a lot lately, but still. That was something they should be able to deal with. If everyone who lived in Lancashire abandoned their responsibilities every time it rained, no one would ever do anything.

Bloody council. As much use as a chocolate fireguard.

She scowled at the names on the headstone, but she shed no tears, and when she couldn't avoid it any longer, she packed up her things and headed back toward the church, collecting a few pieces of paper that were blowing around, and stuffing them purposefully into her bucket.

CHAPTER 6

Preston had to remind himself where he had been going, what he had been planning to do, but once the feel of the tunnel faded behind him, he focused again: the child-killing Brakeman. He was trying to help him. Trying to save him. Maybe the children too, though a possibility had occurred to him as he moved quickly away from the Miley Tunnel.

What if there was a connection between the children the Brakeman had killed and the ones who now haunted the streets and tunnels, singing that bleak and awful song? What if they were one and the same?

If they were, then saving them seemed rather less important than staying away from them. Either way, he had to get to the truth, and that meant visiting the library.

Preston made his way via North Road and Thithebarn Street then down the side of the Guild Hall to the old stone flagged marketplace in the centre of town, the journey taking both an age and no time at all. He climbed the steps of the Harris library into the gloomy lobby where the huge pendulum hung from the ceiling several stories above, unsurprised that the doors opened easily to him though it was night, unsurprised to find the pendulum quite still. He wandered the downstairs rooms where the skeleton of the great elk stood and the Viking sword they'd found in the river, and then he moved up to the floor where they kept the books and found the local history section.

But he could not get in. He had been here once before, years ago, but that, apparently, was not enough. He could see it, its shelves of musty volumes and the card catalogue in wooden drawers, but the air around it was solid. Realising once more just how much of the town was cut off to him because he had not visited it enough in life, he felt a pang of loss and failure.

He was turning to go back down the long and stately staircase with its heavy wooden rail and stone balustrade when something stopped him. There was a painting above the stairs, a seated woman in yellow, young and beautiful, whose piercing eyes followed you round the room. It was a frank, interested look that made him feel . . . what? Curious? Exposed, certainly, but also intrigued by her level, penetrating gaze that reminded him vaguely of the girl with the chestnut hair. But then, even as he stood there considering, there came something else, something quite different, that reminded him of standing at the mouth of the Miley Tunnel and looking in to its cold blackness. The feeling deepened sharply and Preston took a step backwards as the picture began to move. The image in the frame was throbbing, swirling into sinister life. Something was coming through the picture. Something awful.

He stared at the woman in the painting, and her face began to change so that any resemblance to the girl who now lived in his house was sloughed off like old skin. The eyes darkened and hollowed, the lower jaw grew slack, and the figure lurched suddenly upright. It grasped the edge of the picture frame with long, pale fingers, and then it was growing as it climbed out. The feet were pale and bare, and Preston had a sudden and terrible memory of the figure which had attacked him the night his watch stopped, the night he had died. There was no doubt in his mind. The Bannister Doll was back, though it looked quite different, it was here and crawling out of the old picture frame, its dead eyes fastened on him. It had picked up his scent at the Miley Tunnel and had followed him here to finish what it had begun.

Wide eyed, he backed against the rail and felt the great library's vaulted ceilings swimming above him. He fought to control his balance, and then stumbled backwards down

one step, then another. He righted himself and forced his eyes away from the dreadful creature which had left the portrait and was walking unsteadily towards him. Preston looked down the stairs and took a deliberate step. The thing behind him was moving faster now, as if driven by a clear sense of terrible purpose.

It still had something of the woman in the portrait but it was changing all the time, growing bulky and grotesque so that it had begun to shamble like an upright bear. The face was still the woman's: a hard, sculpted beauty now distorting as it grew longer, the eyes sunken, gleaming hard and black as beads. The feet were still bare and small, like a child's, but the eyes weren't eyes anymore. The lashes had grown long and hard like the spines that surround a Venus flytrap, and the eyes were now gaping, widening until they threatened to split the face open and blur into each other. Inside them was a dark, swirling void that Preston could feel pulling at him, leeching away his hope, his will to survive. The Doll gaped wider still, the lower jaw falling down to its chest and below, so that what had been a mouth was now impossibly broad, a great sucking hole like a tunnel into nothingness, out of which drifted the faint notes of an echoing song.

"Oh, don't deceive me.
Oh, never leave me . . ."

Preston forced himself to take another step back, overwhelmed by a wild longing to be anywhere that was not here, surrounded by light and people. His desperation spiked. He needed to be somewhere else, but there was nowhere to go where she wouldn't get him. Unless . . . ?

He focused hard and suddenly the world shifted, flickering with colour, with filtered sunlight. And there were people. Not ghosts but living people, their voices swirling and echoing indistinctly. He saw an old woman with a hair net and a shopping bag, a family with two girls in sopping rain coats, and a man in uniform watching them severely. They weren't quite solid, and the sounds which broke upon him seemed to be drifting in from somewhere far away, but they were real, and Preston knew without a shadow of a doubt that he was seeing the world of the living again.

The ghastly apparition which had been pursuing him was gone, so he stood quite still, smelling the new air with its notes of old books and rain and furniture polish. It seemed like a very long time since he had smelled anything at all. He almost closed his eyes, but he did not dare for fear it would all be gone when he reopened them, so he was looking directly at the man in uniform when Preston saw him flinch. The guard's eyes were focused on the space where Preston stood.

"You can see me!" he gasped. "You know I'm here."

The man gaped, but he looked puzzled as if he wasn't sure what he was looking at. He moved his head from side to side, eyes locked on Preston's, but the more Preston willed him to say something, the more the man's gaze unfixed. He blinked, cleared his throat uncertainly, and then went back to watching the two girls whose coats were dripping on his nice clean floor.

In the same instant, Preston felt the colours fading, the sound receding. He ran down the stairs and out the great doors before the world returned to the grey twilight he knew so well. He kept moving through his exhaustion, hurrying around the corner to the ornate buildings of Miller Arcade, checking behind him that there was no sign of the spectre which had stalked him, the thing he felt sure had been the Bannister Doll, whatever it had looked like. He should have been relieved, should have wanted to sing with the delight of escaping whatever horrors would have engulfed him if the Doll had caught him up in that terrible mouth of hers, but the world of the living which he had briefly glimpsed, was gone, and he felt only lost and alone.

* * *

The Leech howled its fury. The boy was more accomplished than it had expected. If it had anticipated his fleeing into the present like that the Leech would have moved with him with barely an effort. But it had been surprised and in that split second of confusion, the boy had slipped away. Next time, it resolved in its dark, chill heart, it would not be so easily dodged. Next time, the Leech would feed.

* * *

Preston wandered the town's deserted streets, from the flag market across Cheapside and into Friargate, then through St. George's shopping centre where he had whiled away Saturday afternoons in Ames' record shop, over Fishergate and down to Avenham Park where he had seen the ghost Romans. He would stay on this side of the river so as not to risk running into them again, but he had to be alert to the world so he wouldn't lose any more of it. And besides, he needed to be on his guard for when the Doll came hunting him.

Hunting.

He wasn't sure where that word came from, but he immediately felt sure it was right. The encounter in the library had been no coincidence. The Doll was looking for him, trying to finish what it had started. Preston thought of that awful, gaping mouth, and walked quickly through the dark gardens with their great mounding screens of rhododendron. In life he would have been scared to be alone here at night, and it had been a small relief that with death had come a kind of safety. There was, after all, no one around to hurt him, and what could happen to him that was worse than death? But Roarer's dark warnings and the encounter in the library had shaken this conviction. He didn't know what the Bannister Doll could do to him, but then he didn't know how a ghost had been able to kill him in the first place, and he felt in his bones that to be pulled into the creature's terrible mouth wouldn't just be the end of even the half-life he knew now. What it would be, he couldn't say, but it felt like . . . what did they say in the old films?: A fate worse than death?

Sounds about right.

He recalled the awful moment he had died, the eyes of the barefoot spectre holding him, its hand reaching into his chest and suddenly becoming solid enough to close about his heart. What could be worse than that?

Something. He sensed it as he might once have sensed the damp cold of fog when his eyes were shut. The Doll wasn't finished with him, and having felt its malice, what it had in store for him could only be dreadful, whether he could imagine it or not.

He shuddered and pushed the thought away, moving through the little gate into the Japanese garden where he had used to sit and watch the koi in the pond, and he tried to make sense of what had happened, and what he had learned. Two things, he decided. The Doll was a shape shifter of some kind, a spirit which could take different forms. The second thing was that the guard in the museum had seen him, like the girl in his bedroom.

Roarer had been right. This was his gift, and though he could use it to find out stuff that might help him and others escape this endless moment, he could also use it to re-join the living: move among them. If he got really good at it, maybe it would almost be like being alive again.

Preston looked around and tried to imagine the garden in daylight, with little children picking their way through the shrubs and gazing rapt at the bright orange fish. He pictured adults resting on benches and, in the field beyond which ran down towards the river, kids in school uniforms kicking a ball about. He had seen all these things in this very spot. Now he closed his eyes and willed it all back.

He paused, then opened his eyes.

There was the merest flicker of colour, a smear of green and red like the afterimage of a bright light, and then there was just the darkened garden again. He repeated the process, squeezing his eyes shut and reaching out with his mind like he was a storybook magician summoning power, but when he opened them again there was nothing. Twice more he tried, but his conviction was gone and he couldn't manage even that flicker of colour. His mind was tired, and he just didn't want it badly enough.

Miserable, he walked down to the river and sat on the grass, watching the water where it moved broad and dark beneath the pylons of the old railway bridge. After a while he rose, checked the display on his watch out of habit (nine twenty-two) and set off home again. He saw no one, living or dead, until he had completed the long slow journey, thinking of the girl who lived there now and who might be able to see him.

CHAPTER 7

The girl in question, Tracey Blenkinsop, was sitting in the room which had been Preston's, listening to the radio, trying to decide what she thought of Madness's 'Baggy Trousers' whose manic video she'd seen on *Top of the Pops*. The next song up, Hazel O'Connor's 'Eighth Day,' was easier to like because it was cool and deep and silly all at the same time. They were just into the first chorus when she saw the ghost boy.

He sort of faded into the room, like the last shot of a film in reverse, so that she saw him grow distinct right in front of her, his face tight with focus, so that she was sure he was somehow making his materialisation happen. Except that it wasn't really materialisation because he never became solid, and the details of his form were blurry as if he was being sketched in the air with water colour.

But *colour* was wrong too. The boy was a shifting column of grey tones, smearing into black in some parts (the nostrils, the circles under his brooding eyes) and white in others (the skin of his cheek, the uneven gleam of his pale hair), with other colours, such as the pallid green of his shirt, barely registering. He looked like part of an old and badly preserved photograph. His mouth was moving and his eyes were focused on her, but she could hear nothing.

Without taking her eyes off the apparition, Tracey reached behind her and silenced Hazel O'Connor, but there was still no sound from the ghost's earnestly moving lips.

"What do you think you are doing here?" she demanded, doing her best to ignore the sudden thumping of her heart. "This is my room. No one comes in here without my permission."

The boy's mouth continued to move.

"I can't hear you," she said, irritably. "What is it?"

The boy seemed to grow misty as if he were disappearing, but then – with another obvious effort of will – came back.

"Stay!" Tracey insisted. "I'm not done talking to you."

She considered his shadowed eyes.

"Can you even hear me?" she demanded, tapping her ear with one hand.

The ghost seemed to flicker and something came into

its face that might have been confusion. Its palms opened and its head shook slightly.

No. It could see her, but it couldn't hear her.

"What are you doing here?" she mouthed. "I'm not afraid of you, you know. Am I supposed to be? Are you here to scare me, because if you are, you're gonna have to do better than this."

The ghost shook his head, but the eyes held something uncertain.

"Oh," said Tracey. "Right. Well, if there's something you want you're going to have to find a way to tell me."

The ghost's almost colourless lips moved again, but there was still no sound.

"Who are you anyway?" asked Tracey. "Why are you dressed like that? Have I met you before? You seem . . . No, better question: what are you?" she asked. "I mean," she adjusted realising she could not hear what the boy said in response, "are you a ghost?"

She mouthed the word carefully and pointed at him until he understood. The boy hesitated, his face suddenly awash with powerful and complicated feeling which resolved into sadness. He nodded once, but just as she felt she was on the edge of recognising him the image began to fade and flicker again. The boy's eyes closed and he gritted his teeth. For a moment he seemed to clarify again so that his outline hardened for a second, but he could not sustain whatever energy it took to keep him there, and his features grew vague again, cloudy. A moment later, he was gone.

"Who were you talking to?"

Tracey wheeled to see her mother's head stuck round the door.

"What?" she replied, flustered. "No one. I was just . . . Don't you knock?"

Preston collapsed exhausted on his bedroom floor, then pounded his hands on the carpet in frustration so that the dark house echoed. He had been so close. Another few moments and he felt sure he could have made the girl hear him. But the effort required was so great, the deep and swelling weariness he felt in every bone and muscle of his Merely Dead body so overwhelming, that he couldn't see how he would ever last more than a few seconds.

He wasn't sure why it seemed so important to talk to the girl who lived in his room in what he couldn't help but think of as the future, though he knew it was really the present, albeit her present, not his. What he had really gone back for was the *Myths and Legends* book he had seen her reading. If he could look through it he felt sure he could learn something about the Brakeman and the children connected to his death. His instinct said that the more he knew, the closer they would all be to escaping this half-life forever.

But the girl had gotten into his head. He had known it was a possibility that she would be there, but confronted with the fact of it he had lost sight of his purpose, had almost forgotten about the book, in his sudden and desperate desire to connect to an actual living person. Of course, he had never been able to talk to girls when he had been alive, and had actually failed to talk to this very girl moments before he died, so why he thought he would be able to do it now made no sense at all.

Somehow, however, he had to. *Needed* to.

Because though he didn't know her, though a part of him resented her for being in his house, and though she was a girl from a completely different world than him, she was his best link to the world of the living and all it represented. She was alive, her blood pumping, her eyes wet when she cried. She tired when she ran, healed when she bruised, grew and aged and looked forward to a future when the world and her place in it would be different. All this touched a sense of longing in Preston, a yearning to share her life that was jealous and joyous and sad all at once. He sat alone in the dim light, staring up at the plastic aircraft he knew had been thrown away years ago, and he felt the sting of loneliness.

But the longer he sat there, the more feeling sorry for himself felt both inadequate and a little shoddy. Having failed at the library, Preston had crossed over to see the *Myths and Legends* book in the hope that he could help the Brakeman whose sense of self was dissolving. He had not done so, and that meant that he had to go back.

He waited another minute or so, building his strength, and then he stood beside the bed. *His* bed, though it was in the same spot as hers was. Would be. Whatever. He closed his eyes and opened his mind.

It took longer this time, because he had not fully recovered from before, and he had to wrap his consciousness around the image of the girl's present like a hand closing its grip around a climbing rope. When he opened his eyes, he thought it hadn't worked, because the room was still dark, but then he realised that the walls were pink and purple, but the lights were out and the sun had set. What had been seconds to him had been hours to her. And now she was asleep in the bed.

For a moment he just looked at her, embarrassed, but inexplicably pleased to see her, so that he had to remind himself what he had come for. The book was on her bedside table. He reached for it, felt the soft brush of something half solid beneath his fingers, and concentrated harder until the cover became firm and crisp under his hand. He opened it carefully and scanned the title page. Mid way down he found the entry he sought:

The Railway Man's Ghost. Page 33.

Excited, Preston began to turn the pages, but it was difficult, and as he tired, the paper seemed to slip through his fingers. He thumbed roughly, hopefully, but guessed wrong and had to turn back eight pages. He could feel the energy of his mind draining away. He tried to get a firmer hold on himself, turned another page, and then the book was slipping through his hands and falling to the floor.

He cried out, and in that instant the girl awoke. She saw the fallen book, saw him, and gasped. Then, recovering her composure, she snatched the book from the floor and held it out towards him, a question in her face.

"Which page?" she said.

The words were so clear that, for a moment, he thought he had actually heard them, but when he answered her brow furrowed with confusion. He repeated it, urgent – "Thirty-three!" – over and over though he knew she could not hear him. And then, just as his despair was pushing him back into his own world, he saw her eyes lock onto his lips as he spoke, and she understood.

Her hands flew over the book, flipping pages until she got to a two-page spread with an inexpertly sketched image of a grizzled-looking man standing inside an open topped railway wagon, stacked with hunks of rock.

"This?" she mouthed, holding it up for him to see.

He nodded, but his eyes were already scanning the text,

trying to make sense of the account as his grip on her world finally became impossible to sustain. He faded back into his own time, his face alive with triumph, relief and something like gratitude for the girl who was unafraid of him.

* * *

Preston found the Brakeman as soon as he had the strength to walk, but he had to go past his old school, through Grimsargh and all the way to Longridge to do so. The Brakeman was pacing the old line, oil lamp held high, muttering through his catalogue of duties as ever. He did not react to Preston's approach, did not appear to see him at all, and when Preston reached out and touched him on his elbow he merely hesitated, like a man stirring in his sleep without actually waking. Preston tapped him twice, purposefully, but still the man merely whispered his usual litany.

"Check the brakes on't wagons, check that the points are set, check the wagon loads are stable."

"Listen," said Preston. "I know who you are. I know what happened and why you are here."

"Check the brakes on't wagons," muttered the Brakeman, walking down the track. "Check that the points are set . . ."

"No," said Preston, running to catch up and striking the Brakeman in the small of his back with his fist.

The man stumbled and turned dreamily, but whatever thought had been there evaporated before he completed the revolution to where Preston stood.

"Check the wagon loads are stable," he muttered, resuming his walking.

Preston went after him, reaching for the glass of the oil lamp. He found the release catch and forced the glass shade up. The Brakeman's body seemed to respond to the pressure, but his eyes barely flickered.

"Check the brakes on't wagons," he muttered.

Preston stooped and blew out the lamp flame.

For a moment it was like the Brakeman had been unplugged. He just stopped where he was, and for a brief, terrible moment, Preston thought he might have somehow killed the ghost for real. But then the Brakeman's head turned slowly towards the lamp and his eyes, which had been unfixed, focused. His face began to change, the bland earnestness turning into a desperate and terrifying horror. The familiar string of words dried up, and in their place came a low, dragging moan of dread and grief. It took Preston a second to realise that there were words within the sound, or rather one word repeated.

"No. No. No," said the Brakeman. "I can't reach. If I could just . . . reach."

Preston was seized by the possibility that he had

made a terrible mistake, that he had somehow plunged the Brakeman into some new private hell, but he forced himself to speak.

"It's all right," he said. "There's no trains out here. Not anymore."

"No," echoed the Brakeman, his stricken face staring at the dead lantern. "No."

"It's all right," Preston insisted, catching some of the other's desperation. "There's no danger. The trains are all safe. You can stop now."

"No," said the Brakeman. And then, to Preston's surprise, he added, "Never stop. Must never stop."

"You can," said Preston, seizing the moment. "You can stop. It's safe now."

"Never stop," said the Brakeman, suddenly sounding desperately tired. "If I stop, there are accidents. People die."

"I know," said Preston. "I know what happened. 1859. You were bringing a load of stone from the quarry in Longridge, remember? The brakes on the first wagon failed. You tried to climb back to the next one but the train was picking up speed. As you reached for the brakes on the second wagon, you fell and died under the wheels."

Preston waited but the Brakeman said nothing and seemed momentarily frozen, lost in his own memories. Preston had hoped he wouldn't have to say the next part, but the Brakeman was stuck, entranced. He had to hear the end of the story.

"The line slopes down from Longridge," said Preston, in a voice barely above a whisper. "Without the brakes, the wagons picked up speed. They should have been slowed, stopped and shunted into a siding, but no one saw them coming until it was too late. They were doing sixty miles an hour when they slammed into the half past six train coming up the line from Preston."

"A passenger train," said the Brakeman, his voice hollow as his eyes.

Preston blinked, then looked down.

"I'm sorry," he said.

"The first carriage was annihilated," said the Brakeman, lucid now, but staring off, as if seeing something far away. "Nothing left. It had been bringing . . ." he hesitated, and for a long moment said nothing at all, so that Preston looked up into his face. It was still blank, but Preston had the impression of some terrible struggle going on under the surface. "It had been bringing a school party home after a day in town," the Brakeman concluded. "One survivor," he said, his eyes wide as if he was seeing them again for the first time. "A girl. The others . . . Twelve dead."

Twelve, Preston thought. Were they singing an old English folksong about a wronged maiden in the valley at the moment of impact? Was that the connection? And if so, what had happened to them after the accident?

"My fault," the old ghost continued. "I am the Brakeman."

"You were," said Preston. "And you did what you could that day, and lost your life in the process but . . ."

"I am the Brakeman."

"Yes," said Preston, gripping the man by his arm, "but before that you were just a man. Your name was Josiah Edmund Jones and you have been dead for almost one hundred and twenty years."

There was silence. The Brakeman's eyes half closed and opened again.

"I am . . ." he said, and faltered. "I am . . ."

"Josiah Edmund . . ." Preston began.

"Jones," said the Brakeman. He breathed, or seemed to, a long shuddering breath as if he had been holding it in and now drank in the cool night air. It brought life to his face. "I tried," he said. "God knows I tried. I just couldn't reach . . ."

As he spoke, something happened. The mouth of the cutting ahead of them which had been a yawning charcoal-coloured maw, rippled and vanished. In its place was a smoke-stained brick wall with a green door, the brass handle badly tarnished. The Brakeman's eyes slid to it and focused, his perplexed expression gradually chased away by realisation and something else which might have been relief, even joy.

"My door," he said. "My home."

Preston stepped aside, his eyes wide, unsure what was happening, but guessing, hoping, praying that his instinct was right.

The Brakeman took two slow steps towards it, then two more a little faster, and as he moved, the lantern lowered, forgotten. He reached his hand to the latch, turned it and pressed, his eyes closing in anticipation. As the door opened, he gave a little gasping sigh that might have been a sob, and then he turned to Preston, his eyes shining.

"I don't know what you'll find if you go through," said Preston, suddenly afraid.

"That doesn't matter," said Josiah Edmund Jones. "Thank you."

He smiled and stepped slowly, purposefully into the doorway.

"Wait," called Preston. "The children who died. What happened to them after . . . ?"

But the old man was already closing the door behind him. As it latched shut, it flickered out of existence, and there was only the mouth of the cutting and the shadows of the railway embankment.

Preston waited but he knew the Brakeman would not

come back, that he was gone for ever into whatever awaited the Sincerely Dead. He stared at the deserted track unsure what to feel. His pride wrangled with a jealousy that he had not passed over with the Brakeman, though he also felt the bone-deep surety that – unlike him – Preston was not ready. He was terrified to the core of his being at what may lie beyond that little wooden door. He wondered if the entrance would look different for other people, for him, if he would ever see it again, and if he would ever have the courage, the certainty, to go through it.

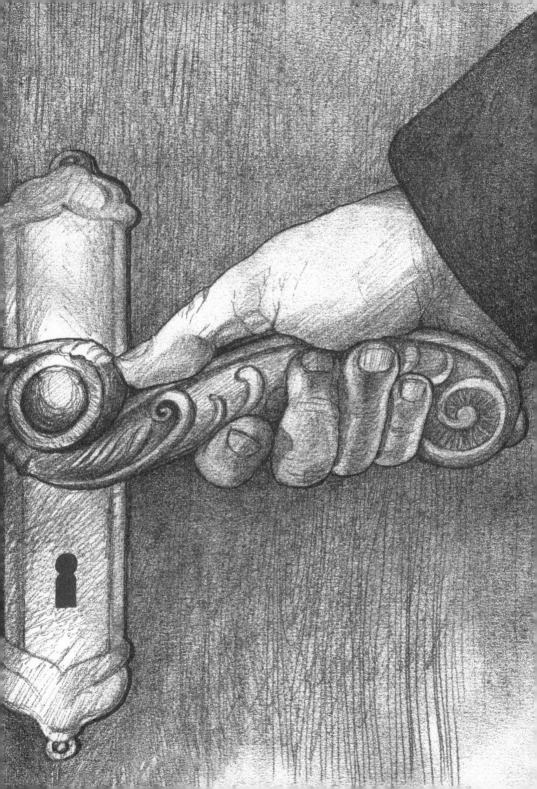

CHAPTER 8

Tracey had read the account of the Brakeman's death several times over the next two days, absorbing the horror of the thing. Twelve dead not including the Brakeman, and only one little girl who walked away from the first carriage. What terrors would that child carry with her for the rest of her life? It was no wonder the Brakeman had haunted the spot ever since. She wondered what it was that made a ghost. Must it always be something so appalling, and if so what had happened to the boy she had seen in her room? She shuddered, but the horrible possibilities gave way to an altogether different realisation.

Strange, she thought. She believed in ghosts. Just like that. A week ago she didn't, and now she did. Seeing really was believing.

She closed the little book and went down to the kitchen

where her father was sitting in an easy chair, his face buried in the *Lancashire Evening Post*.

"Dismal," Tracey's dad pronounced.

"What is?" asked Tracey, warily. If the answer had anything to do with politics she knew she would regret asking, but she was fairly sure he had been reading the back page and that meant . . .

"North End," he said, folding the paper up and slapping it down on the floor.

The once great team of the legendary Tom Finney, now languishing in the lower half of the third division.

"Lost three nil to Swansea City," he mused. "Hopeless."

"Away?" she asked, peering at the paper.

"Aye," he conceded, "but since they've only won four times at home all season that's not much of a consolation, is it?"

"I suppose not," Tracey agreed, reaching for the paper. She had learned long ago that where talking to her father about football was concerned, the trick was to sound sympathetic and say as little as possible. Discussion only encouraged him. She flipped the paper over so that the offending sports page was no longer visible, scanned the front page, then turned to the next. She caught her breath. The headline read, "Housewife sees Railway Spectre!"

She read hungrily. The story was no more than a

few sentences and a pair of photographs, one of a hefty middle-aged woman trying to hold her stomach in, the other a stretch of the railway line as it went through a rocky cutting with a metal bridge. The gist was simple enough. A woman called Hattie Richardson, who lived in Longridge, had been returning home from the chippie with 'a fish supper' for her husband and herself, when she was startled by a curious sight on the railway line below the road. As she had been crossing the bridge her attention had been caught by a sudden flash of light 'a bit like a firework' which had illuminated a man in old-fashioned uniform overalls carrying an unlit oil lamp. The man had stood there for a moment, as if in conversation, and then stepped into the cutting, at which point the light had flickered out and the man had vanished. Mrs. Richardson checked both sides of the bridge but the man did not emerge. The apparition matched the description of a ghostly railway worker long since reported to haunt the area, though no new sightings had been reported for many years.

Tracey reread the story twice, then stared out of the window, seeing nothing.

"What?" said her father. He leaned across to see what she had been reading and made a dismissive noise. "People will do owt to get in't paper. Where you off to?"

"Homework," said Tracey, the one thing no one in the Blenkinsop household would ever question.

She left the room and moved quietly into the lounge where the phone sat on a delicate table with a souvenir saucer from Staines. She pulled out the directory and flicked through the thin pages. P. Q. R, for Richardson. She couldn't find a Hattie, but she did find a Bob and H. Richardson with a Longridge address. She considered dialling the phone number, but thought better of it, and wrote the address down instead.

Back in the kitchen her father gave her a thoughtful look.

"I thought you were doing homework?" he said.

"I have to get a book from Carol's," she said. "I won't be long."

It was too far to walk, and the bus was pulling into the stop at the top of Moorfield Drive just as she got there. She checked her pockets for the fare, and strode aboard, climbing the tight spiral steps to the upper deck and coughing at the grey haze of cigarette smoke. Twenty-five minutes later she was trying the doorbell of Mrs. Hattie Richardson.

The picture hadn't done the sheer bulk of the woman justice, and Tracey suspected the paper had used what the woman had given them – something from a few years earlier, probably – rather than sending their own photographer.

"Mrs. Richardson?" said Tracey. "I'm sorry to bother you. My name is Tracey Blenkinsop and I'm doing a school project on local legends."

The idea had come to her on the bus. She had thought perhaps she should come up with something less direct, but this seemed easier and less likely to get her caught in a tangle of lies.

"Ooh," said Hattie Richardson, lighting up like she'd won the football pools. "You'd better come in."

The hallway was narrow and smelled of old pie crust, with almost as much stale cigarette smoke as there had been on the bus. Tracey followed Hattie's great wobbling girth through to the kitchen, squeezing past shelves of china shepherdesses and cherubs, to where the lady of the house took up position behind an ironing board piled with laundry. The Carpenters' 'Yesterday Once More' was playing on the radio. Tracey's mother always cried at that song, something they were so used to that it had become a family joke even her mother laughed at through her tears.

"You'll be wanting to know about my encounter," said Hattie, lighting up a cigarette and looking pleased with herself.

"I read the newspaper article," said Tracey.

"Article," echoed Hattie with a dismissive snort of

cigarette smoke that made her look like a steam locomotive. "They barely gave me two words."

"What did they leave out?" asked Tracey, sitting on the edge of the chair to which Mrs. Richardson had waved her with one meaty hand.

"Well, I didn't stick around once I was sure he'd disappeared because mi mushy peas were getting cold," she said, with formal care, "but I was fairly sure there was someone with 'im."

"Another ghost, you mean?" said Tracey.

"Right and correct," said Hattie. "I didn't get much of a look at 'im, but it were a boy. Struck me as odd because he looked like he were wearing a uniform. Army, I thought, at first. Later on, mind, once I'd 'ad a cup of tea and were able to collect meself, like, I thought it were more like . . ." "A Scout," said Tracey, realising in the moment she said it. In the same instant the memory finally came back to her: a boy walking in the dark on Ribbleton Avenue, a boy who had avoided her eyes. It was him. She was sure of it.

Hattie stared at her.

"Now 'ow did you know that?" she asked.

Tracey blinked.

"It's a feature of some of the legends," she answered, blushing as she improvised. "The Brakeman and the Scout, they call it. Most people just talk about the Brakeman, but the most reliable accounts," she said carefully, "like yours, include the Scout."

Hattie drew on the cigarette and nodded, proud to be one of the reliable ones.

"He 'ad a big round badge right here," she said, patting her front up by her left shoulder.

"Yes," said Tracey, remembering the detail for the first time. "White with a kind of crest on it. A crown, maybe."

"I weren't close enough to see," said Hattie. "But I remember there were a badge."

Tracey tried to recall the night she had seen the boy, quietly amazed she remembered him at all. She had been with her parents, house hunting. That meant it was two years ago. She wondered how long after that moment the boy had died, and the curiosity and excitement which she had been riding shifted suddenly into pity for what the boy had lost.

"Mrs. Richardson," Tracey added. "Are you a medium?"

Hattie paused in her drag, and shook her head sadly.

"A large, love," she said. "Always 'ave been."

"I mean," Tracey clarified, trying not to giggle, "do these kind of things happen to you often – sort of, supernatural things, ghosts, spirits and what have you?"

"Never before," said Hattie. She grew thoughtful and then her face split into a grin, after which she threw back her head and shrieked with laughter. "Oh! A *medium*!" she cackled. "I've always bin a large!"

* * *

Preston had expected a greater sense of resolution to come from what he had done for the Brakeman, he had even thought it would point his own way somehow, but with the Brakeman gone and no new information about the children who had died with him, there just seemed to be one less thing to distract him from his predicament. He thought a lot about the girl, who lived in his house, particularly when he couldn't find Roarer or had grown tired of his bluster, and he found his mind straying constantly to how life had been before he died, so that he became overwhelmed by the things he had once taken for granted.

Tastes, for instance. He no longer ate at all, and when he tried – sampling a clear cellophane wrapped mint he had found in his pocket – he found it had no flavour and spat it out. But he yearned for the tang of salt and vinegar on hot chips right out of the newspaper. He missed Weetabix. Sausages. Butter pies. Steak and kidney. Hot pot with pickled red cabbage. He missed gorging on Snow Balls and Wagon Wheels from the school tuck shop. He missed the feel of an ice cold can of Coke in his hand on a hot day. Because it wasn't just his taste buds that no longer worked; it was everything that had to do with sensation, pleasurable or otherwise. He couldn't smell anything. He could touch the slick surface of a plastic football, the rough scrape of brick, the softness of fabric and know what they were, but his brain could produce nothing more than knowledge. He felt unaffected by such things, for good or ill. He could feel the blade of a knife, but while the pressure of it against his skin had once felt cold and dangerous, promising pain if he pressed it too much, now he only felt what he knew was metal. It meant nothing to him. So he found that he even missed the pain of a stubbed toe or a paper cut because they had variety. He knew from Roarer's missing fingers that he could damage his body, but unless he did so, everything would be constant and unchanging, presumably forever, and even if he did, he would feel nothing. He would never grow, never see himself as an adult. His body was like his watch, forever stuck at nine twenty-two. That too might once have been appealing to him, though Preston couldn't remember why.

Worst of all, perhaps, was the sense of what he had not done in life and now never could: the girls he wished he had talked to, befriended and more, the guitar he'd never learned to play beyond a few broody chords, the stands he had never taken. He cursed himself for sitting by while Gez Simpson had terrified little Stephen Cummings with his idiot ghost stories, not wanting to draw attention to himself or get into a fight. The young Scout's desperate tears haunted him like an accusation of failure, of cowardice, and there was nothing Preston could do to assuage his guilt. It was too late now. For anything.

Tracey spent two hours in her room with an exercise book and a felt tip pen. She couldn't talk to the ghost Scout, but if she saw him again, she wanted to be ready. She wrote one question on each page in large purple letters, trying to structure each question so that it needed only a yes or no answer. She taped flags to the edges of each page so that she could navigate the questions rapidly, moving swiftly to different subjects depending on the ghost's answers. She didn't understand what she thought of as the *physics* of his appearance, but she knew it took effort on his part and that made for brief visits. If she saw him again, she would waste no time.

Then she got ready for bed – hurriedly, in case he arrived and caught her half-dressed – and waited. When nothing happened, she opened her wardrobe door so she could see the mirror out of the corner of her eye, then selected a book to read. An hour later, her mother poked her head in, demanding why she was still up. Reluctantly, Tracey turned the lights off and went to bed, the exercise book of questions stowed safely under her pillow.

But the night passed without incident, and though she delayed as long as possible before going to school, and went right back to her room as soon as she got home, she got no glimpse of the ghost boy for the entire day, or the next after that. Her disappointment soured like old milk, and she became angry with the boy who had butted into her life and then, apparently, abandoned her, though the moment she recognised her feelings she was annoyed with herself. She had never let any boy occupy her mind like this and she wasn't about to start with one who had been dead for . . .

She realised that she didn't know, but that it would be easy to find out. The Scout uniform would be important, as was the fact that he had visited her in her own room.

"Who lived here before us?" she asked her mother at breakfast.

"A couple called . . ." her mother searched for the name, "Oldcorn," she said. "I don't think we ever met them. Everything went through the estate agent."

"Did they have kids?"

"I don't think so, love. Why?"

"Just wondered," said Tracey, poking at her bacon. "Why did they move?"

Her mother's face clouded but she just shrugged.

"Tough times," she said. "Maybe they thought this house too big for just the two of them. I think they moved to something smaller."

"When you first saw the house," Tracey said, "what was my room like?"

"You know," said her mother, reflectively, "it was funny. The house was completely furnished, of course, every room decorated and crammed with bits and pieces like the people had lived there a long time. But your room was completely empty. The walls were painted white. The carpet was new and the door stuck. It looked like no one had been in for ages, except that . . ." she cast her mind back. "Except that the paint smelled new, like it had just been done. It's not unusual to redecorate before you sell a house, especially if you want a neutral look that will appeal to potential buyers – we did the same at our old place – but it was odd that they only did it to the one room. I remember your dad commenting on it. Still, it meant we had a blank slate: easier to do it up nice for you."

Tracey nodded and smiled.

"Come on," said her mother, checking her watch. "You'll miss the bus."

Preston sat in the old pear tree, his legs dangling, pressing and repressing the button on his watch. Nine twenty-two. Nine twenty-two. Nine twenty-two. In life he had pushed it only occasionally because he knew it would drain the watch's battery, though when he first got it he hadn't been able to resist showing it off. It was unusual for him to have something before everyone he knew had gotten one of their own, and he had enjoyed the attention as the kids at school had, for once, huddled around him, staring at the Texas Instruments time piece, his very own bit of the space age.

"Do it again, Oldcorn," they said. "Let's see it."

The little red square-sided numbers came up and everyone cooed their approval, so that Preston had felt proud and special.

It hadn't lasted, of course. Preston had received the watch as a gift from his parents a year and a half before he died, and within a few months of getting it a new kind of digital watch had appeared. Gez Simpson had one.

"Check it out, Oldcorn!" he'd said. "Permanent display. Not just hours and minutes, but seconds, and a calendar. Cool, huh? I expect you'll want to get one to replace that antique junk of yours. You can't even sell it, can you? Who would pay for that?"

Gez's watch did indeed stay on all the time. It had

little grey numbers. LCD they were called. And it wasn't just Gez Simpson. In no time at all it seemed everyone had one except Preston. He stuck by his clunky old Texas Instruments watch, knowing it would be awkward to ask his parents for a replacement for their gift, amazed and a little sad that something which had seemed so magical could so quickly become an object of scorn. His parents never noticed, and Preston found himself resenting them a little, a feeling that made him feel small and ungrateful.

He gazed at its scratched black face, wondering now if, in this weird no-time, the battery would ever run out no matter how often he pushed the display button. He doubted it and, with a rush of frustration, he went back to pressing it into action.

Nine twenty-two. Nine twenty-two. Nine twenty-two . . .

Still stuck. Still alone. Saving the Brakeman had not helped him or the ghostly children who Preston felt sure had died on the same day, though thoughts of saving them had paled, so unnerved was he by their connection to whatever lived in the Miley Tunnel. Maybe they were beyond saving.

In his heart he knew that he needed to learn more about his own death, as he had learned about the Brakeman's, and that meant researching the one thing he had been trying to avoid. He needed to find out everything he could about the Bannister Doll.

* * *

Tracey had no qualms about approaching Hattie Richardson in person, but the idea of seeking out the Oldcorns and questioning them about the room which was now hers made her very uncomfortable. She spent a whole Saturday afternoon in the reading room of the Harris library going through old copies of the *Lancashire Evening Post* from the months immediately before her parents had bought the house from the Oldcorns, but could find no reference to them or a missing Scout. She wished there was a faster, more efficient way of searching rather than this random scanning of headlines, and eventually approached one of the reference librarians.

"I'm trying to find details of a local murder but I don't know exactly when it happened," she said. "About two years ago, I think."

She wasn't sure why she had said "murder." It had just come out. She wondered if she could qualify the question, say it might not have been a murder, probably wasn't in fact, but the librarian already looked primed not to take her seriously, so she bit the remark back.

Her instinct was right. The librarian was a round-faced man with heavy rimmed spectacles and grey eyes which looked her up and down disapprovingly.

"Rather a strange subject for a young lady to be researching," he said.

"Yeah," said Tracey, deadpan. "I already read all the ponies and rainbow books. Can you help me or not?"

"I can access police records," said the librarian, as if this was against his better judgment. "When did the case go to trial?"

"I don't know that it did."

"What was the name of the victim?"

"I don't know."

The librarian gave her a hard look.

"Maybe Oldcorn," she said.

"In Preston?"

"Yes," she said.

"Wait here."

Tracey stood at the high desk, listening to the respectful silence of the library, watching an old man in a ragged coat, his chair surrounded by shopping bags of clothing, turning the pages of a newspaper which was attached to a long wooden rod. He was unshaven and read with the tip of his tongue poking out from between chapped lips. Homeless, probably, she thought. It seemed like there were more and more of what the papers called 'street people' – like they lived in damp doorways and sodden cardboard boxes out of choice – than there had been when she was small, but maybe that was just because they had moved to a bigger town. Her father would have something to say about it, she reflected, and it would probably have something to do with Margaret Thatcher.

"These are matters of public record," said the librarian, returning with four blue, hard bound volumes lettered in gold. "You can look through their indexes at this desk here. They must not be moved. They must not be marked. I have scrap paper if you need to make notes."

"I have some, thank you," said Tracey.

The volumes had a number of different indexes including one by name of victim. She went through each book, but there were no Oldcorns listed. She returned the books to the librarian, who laid his pen down with studied care, apparently put out that she was done so quickly.

"Could I try missing persons instead?" she ventured.

"Very well," he said, in a way that managed to say that she was imposing on his time.

The missing persons records produced no Oldcorns either.

"What is it exactly that you are trying to achieve?" asked the librarian with heavy condescension.

Tracey scowled and looked down. Something was wrong with her grasp of the facts. Either the boy wasn't called Oldcorn, or he had died in a different time or place. If she was right about those things then he had never been reported missing and had not been murdered. Which left what?

"Hospital records," she tried. "Could I see if a boy of that name was admitted to any of the local . . ."

"Hospital records are kept – amazingly enough – in the respective *hospital*," said the librarian, his lip twitching into the shadow of a satisfied smile. "But they are not public and would only be shown to an immediate family member or a representative of law enforcement. Now, since this is turning into something of a cul-de-sac, I ask that you permit me to get back to my work for other patrons . . ."

"Burial records," said Tracey.

The librarian sighed.

"Which parish? No, let me guess, you don't know . . ."

"Anything in Ribbleton," Tracey said. "And Fulwood."

"Your wish," grumbled the librarian, "is, apparently, my command. This way, please."

He led her into a side office where a machine like a television sat on a desk.

"Have you ever used microfiche before?" asked the

librarian, his bored tone daring her to say "no."

"No," she said. "But it doesn't look hard. Where is the . . ."

"Film?" he said.

"Right," Tracey agreed, as if the word had been on the tip of her tongue.

"Here," said the librarian, indicating a bank of filing cabinets with annotated draws. "Parish records by year and . . ."

"Yes," she inserted. "I get it. I'll call if I need you."

He glared at her and she smiled broadly.

"When you are finished with each roll of film, do not put it back in the filing cabinet. That's how things get lost. Put it here on the desk to be returned by a member of the library staff."

"You," she said.

"Perhaps," he said, grudgingly. He turned imperiously and stalked out.

Tracey got to work.

It took her five minutes to figure out how to thread the film into the machine properly (the right way up) and another three to get a sense of the filing system, but she mastered the system itself in no time. Soon she was flitting through the monochrome display, staring blankly at the columns of names, grumbling that the entries were listed only by date, not by family name. She confined herself to the year before they had moved in to number six, moving from parish to parish without success. She tried the previous year and repeated the painstaking and tedious process, but found no Oldcorns anywhere.

"Making progress?" said the librarian, materialising at her elbow.

"No," said Tracey, avoiding what she knew would be his satisfied smile. "I don't understand it. There's nothing."

"Well, it's closing time anyway," said the librarian, who seemed delighted by the excuse to get her out.

Tracey shouldered her way into her coat and gathered her things together. She walked through to the reading room in surly silence, watching absently as the old man with the shopping bags was shown the door by a watchful security guard.

"That was all the parishes in the area?" she said to the librarian as she was about to step into the grand foyer with the pendulum. "Every one?"

"Of course," said the librarian. "You think our files are incomplete somehow . . . ?" He had begun the remark with a smug and slightly scornful smirk on his round face, but it stalled suddenly, as if something had just occurred to him.

"What?" said Tracey.

"Well," said the librarian, his eyes flicking away from her, "it is all the parishes that share their records with the county authorities."

"Some don't?" said Tracey.

"The Catholic churches don't," said the librarian, still avoiding her gaze.

Tracey's family were nominally C of E. She sighed.

"And you didn't think to mention that despite the fact that Preston is called the most Catholic town in England?"

The librarian's eyes flashed towards her and his mouth opened, but no words came out, and he seemed to freeze, fish-like.

"Great," said Tracey, as she walked away. "That's fabulous."

* * *

Instead of getting off the bus at the top of Cromwell Road, Tracey stayed on down Ribbleton Avenue and got off at the corner of Farringdon Lane. The Catholic church up the road was called Blessed Sacrament.

The front door was locked but around the side she found the entrance to what looked like the priest's house. She tried the doorbell and waited. A woman with a severe face answered the door.

"Yes?"

"I'm sorry to bother you," said Tracey, "but I was wondering if I could see the parish records."

"Now is not a very good time," said the woman. "Perhaps you could come back next week . . ."

"It will only take a moment," said Tracey. "I know exactly what I'm looking for."

That was an exaggeration, but an idea had occurred to her on the bus which she thought would limit her search. The Scout's badge on his uniform had been marked with a crown and – she was fairly sure – dates on either side. The Queen's Silver Jubilee had been in 1977. Her mum had a chipped china mug with a similar emblem on it. Tracey had a vague idea that the Scouts commemorated things like that.

That meant she could probably limit her search to 1978.

"Very well," said the woman, pursing her lips, "but if it takes more than half an hour, you'll have to come back another time."

She led Tracey into a dark, narrow hallway that smelled of incense and detergent, and into a characterless office with a long conference table.

"Are you a nun?" asked Tracey.

The woman raised her eyebrows, but while Tracey suspected she was more amused than affronted it didn't soften the sternness of her features.

"I am Mrs. Macintyre, the housekeeper," she said. "Father Edwards is visiting the Sick."

"Oh," said Tracey, sitting at the pale oak table as directed. "I expect they like that."

The housekeeper gave her a careful look as if she was trying to decide if that had been a joke.

"Clearly you've never met Father Edwards," she remarked, almost under her breath. "Let me see your hands."

Tracey wiped them on her jeans then put them on the table, first palms down, then palms up. The housekeeper scrutinised them.

"I suppose that is in order," she said. "But you shouldn't bite your nails. Most unladylike. What years are you looking for?"

"Late 1977 and 1978," said Tracey.

"Very well. Wait here."

Tracey considered the room with its dozen chairs, its plain crucifix and its frosted glass windows. Since her parents were not religious, she was not used to churches, and had expected something different, something older and more serious. Apart from that whiff of incense in the hallway, the building felt functional, like a well-maintained school room or a business. Actually, she thought, it reminded her of the estate agent's office where her parents had signed the mortgage papers when they bought the house.

The housekeeper returned. She was carrying a single nondescript book with a red ribbon peeking out from its pages.

"The columns are for births, marriages and deaths," she said, opening the book at random. "See? What are you looking for?"

Tracey considered the woman quickly and decided there was no reason to be dishonest.

"I'm trying to find out about a boy who died," she said.

"A boy?" said the housekeeper, her face serious. "How old?"

"I'm not sure," Tracey replied. "About fourteen or fifteen. He was in the Scouts. His name, I think, was . . ."

"Preston Oldcorn," said the housekeeper so quickly that the girl stared. There was something in the woman's eyes, something at first blank with shock, then sharp and watchful, almost wary. "Why him?"

"You knew him?" said Tracey.

For a moment the woman just stared back at her, hard and long, and then she blew out a long breath and her whole body sagged.

"I knew him," she said. "He was an altar boy here. I did the flowers for the funeral. His parents were . . ." she gasped, and turned away, and Tracey was surprised to see her eyes were shining with tears. "They were upset."

Tracey considered the woman and her deliberate, inadequate words thoughtfully. The memory and the grief it had triggered in her had transformed the housekeeper completely, stripped away her bluff and officious outside and shown someone quite different, someone who kept people at a distance but who in her heart of hearts was gentle, even kind. Still, her question, when it came was pointed and her eyes were hard.

"Why are you asking about Preston Oldcorn?" said Mrs. Macintyre.

Tracey met the level gaze and held it.

"He has been visiting me," she said, simply.

The housekeeper stared.

CHAPTER 9

Preston paused as he got used to the light and colour and looked at the room which had once been his. The bed was in the same place as his had been, though the room was so small there weren't many alternatives. He had been to this new present several times now but the shock of it was still acute and biting. The way the stuff of his gloomy but familiar life shifted into this bright and foreign place the moment he stepped through was unsettling and made him feel strangely irrelevant. This time he realised that the room was much lighter than his had ever been because the pear tree that had always shaded the window was gone. He was amazed he hadn't noticed before. Without it the front garden looked small and unfamiliar, so that he wondered – with a rush of anger – why anyone would have cut it down. He gazed from the window over the rain swept garden and for a moment he thought that he was the tree, an absence, the half-memory of a dead past, and for the first time he truly understood that what he was seeing was not the future but a present which had moved on without him.

There was no sign of the girl, and he was surprised to find himself disappointed. He hadn't, after all, come to see her. He had come to look in the *Myths and Legends* book for whatever it might have to say about the Doll. Still, it would have been nice to see her again.

Nice, he decided, wasn't the word, exactly. When he had realised she wasn't there, he had felt a confusion of feelings, amongst which was relief. He hadn't been consciously thinking about her at all, but he had been nervous of being in her presence, then disappointed when he hadn't been. It was curious.

Preston had barely noticed girls at all until he was thirteen. He had been aware of them but they had held no power over his imagination, not when there were models to build, books to read, or trips to see *Star Wars* at the Odeon by himself. But something odd had happened in the first week of secondary school.

St. John Southworth had felt vast and intimidating, and he had clung to the half friendships he had with the kids who had been at his primary school like they were life belts on a deep and turbulent sea. Anyone he knew even slightly from Blessed Sacrament he treated as a close friend and, for the most part, since all but the toughest and coolest felt the same way, they reciprocated. One of them was a girl who had been in his class at the old school called Janet Littlechild. He hadn't known her especially well, and only approached her out of a need to surround himself with familiar faces, but she had smiled at him, and asked him about his summer. As they were about to part to go to lessons, she had put one hand on his upper arm and squeezed it in a friendly sort of way, and something strange happened. The light struck her pale, translucent skin, her mouth became perfect – soft and pink – and her dark eyes had sudden depths to them so that he thought he might fall into them. His words evaporated, and he just stood there, smiling vaguely, until she moved on to greet someone else.

Her face, it turned out, was not just familiar. It was beautiful.

Whether it had always been so, and he had simply not noticed it before, or if she had changed over the summer, Preston could not decide. He also didn't know what it meant, this curious power she suddenly had over him, though he knew the words the other kids used. Jimmy Vary had said he *fancied* her, but that didn't sound right. *Love* was too grand as well, and in truth the whole thing passed within a few short weeks, lasting barely longer than it had taken for Preston to realise that Janet had adjusted to being at Southworth rather better than he had, which meant she had gone back to not noticing he existed. Maybe if he'd had a sharp-looking leather jacket to sling on over his uniform she would have paid him more attention, but he doubted it. There had been a few painful days where he had felt lost and upset for reasons he couldn't explain to himself and wouldn't dream of discussing with anyone else, and then it had passed.

What hadn't passed was his shyness which, in the presence of girls, had become embarrassing. In that moment when he had realised Janet Littlechild was beautiful something of his childhood had left him and it had taken his voice with it. Though his feelings for her had gradually faded, his voice hadn't come back, not really, and most of the time when girls spoke to him he just nodded and grunted and laughed, like an idiot. If he found the girl even slightly interesting or attractive he turned into a stumbling fool, incapable of framing the simplest meaningful sentence, so that he started to dread seeing girls at all, afraid that they would see his cringing, stupid embarrassment like a sign around his neck.

Over the summer he had met a perky blonde girl called Yvonne when he had been out sketching by the canal. She wore faded jeans, tight across her bum, and her curly hair smelled faintly of vanilla. She'd been with a mate, Sandra, and had been – he felt sure – interested in him. They saw each other every few days for two weeks, meeting as if by accident, much to the amusement of the worldlier, eye-rolling Sandra. He had liked Yvonne, but had been incapable of holding the simplest conversation and, since she wasn't much better at it, they had somehow managed to part without ever making it beyond small talk or – and this seemed hard to believe – exchanging phone numbers.

He had barely known her, but the moment it was clear he would never see her again he had begun to brood silently on the memory of those days by the canal. In time, of course, the frustrated yearning when he thought about her had faded, and when he tried to remember the feeling it was like something he'd read about, something that had happened to someone else. So he wasn't sure why Yvonne's face had come into his mind now, as he stood in the room which had been his, but he recognised the curious electric leak of disappointment that the girl with the chestnut hair who lived in the room now was not there.

He frowned and pushed the thought away.

The *Myths and Legends* book was on the bed. He reached for it with mind and fingers, lifting the cover to the contents page. He was getting better at it. He glanced down the list, then turned to the second page and saw it under a section on Marsh Lane, the Miley Tunnel and the street whose name had seemed so ominous before, Cold Bath Street.

"The Banister Doll."

Of course it was there. Of course the ghost was somehow connected to the tunnel and to Cold Bath Street. He had somehow known that already.

But for a moment the room swam and he thought he would slip back into his own time, but he fought it, gripping the book to anchor him, then fumbling for the page. The line drawing showed a man in a tall hat pulling a young woman by the hair, a rod or cane in his free hand.

Gez Simpson's versions of the story had never been the same from one telling to the next, and his narrative had fastened on sightings of the blood-streaked spectre and the terrible things she would do to those who saw her. So far as Preston could remember, neither Gez nor anyone else had ever said much about the woman who, in death, had become the Bannister Doll, except that she had been murdered.

Preston read the story, and when it was done, he sank onto the bed and kept very still for a long time, barely noticing when the pop singer poster turned back into his bird chart, and his ceiling was repopulated by his old Spitfires and Hurricanes. He felt drained, and not just from the effort of staying in the world of the living.

The boys in the Scouts had assumed that the banister in Bannister Doll had something to do with the manner of her death. Some said she had been hanged from the rail at the top of the staircase. Other accounts said she had been tied to the banister and beaten to death. It had never occurred to Preston that Bannister might just be her name.

So was Doll. Again, the Scouts' stories had tried to make sense of the title by making the girl look like a doll, or by giving her one which she carried around and left in the rooms of her victims before she struck. Dolls were creepy and added to the mood of the story, especially those with the hard porcelain faces and the glass eyes that opened.

But the truth – if the book could be trusted – was simpler. The girl at the heart of the story had been one Dorothy Bannister – Doll or Dolly for short. She was the daughter of John Bannister, a powerful Preston man who, around 1700, ran the grim House of Correction which had been built on the site of the medieval Franciscan Friary along what was now Marsh Lane, a stone's throw from the oddly, ominously titled Cold Bath Street. Preston remembered talking about the tunnel to Roarer. What had he said when Preston had asked him where the track led?

"The station. *Eventually.*"

But that eventually had been loaded, a strange and fearful dodge of something the other boy hadn't wanted to talk about, something at the end of the Miley Tunnel before the lines wound on to the main station.

Cold Bath Street?

Perhaps.

Preston scowled, then turned his focus back to the story he had just read. John Bannister had been a hard, volatile man, used to dealing with criminals, a man who stood on his dignity and that of his family. When his daughter confessed that, though she was unmarried, she was to have a baby, her father, fearing scandal and shame was to descend upon his house, flew into a towering rage. He dragged the terrified girl outside and publicly beat her to death. Only afterwards did Bannister learn that his daughter had been raped, and though he grieved for what he had done, it was too late to save her, and she was buried in Holy Trinity churchyard.

The rest of the account concerned itself with the Doll's subsequent terrifying attacks on the living, but for once they did not frighten Preston, and not only because he was now a ghost himself. For one thing, the tales of the haunting sounded wrong, not so very far removed from Gez's embellishments, featuring clanking chains and a vengeful female spectre who targeted young men and beat them, bloodily, to death. Nothing about them suggested the strange barefoot horror which had attacked him or the manner in which it had taken his life. But Preston's confused feelings came also from the way Dorothy Bannister had died and the monstrous injustice done by the man who should have loved her most. He had expected to be afraid of what he read about the phantom which had killed him. He had not expected to pity her.

* * *

Mrs. Macintyre, the church housekeeper, ran Tracey home in an ancient sky-blue Triumph Herald whose wheel arches were eaten away with rust. She had said little since Tracey had revealed the source of her interest in the dead Oldcorn boy, but her face was sombre and she had not dismissed the girl's story as ridiculous.

"It's this one on the left," said Tracey, as they pulled midway down Langdale Road.

The housekeeper eased the car over, pulled hard on the hand break and turned the engine off.

"I'll see you to the door," she said.

Tracey gave her a quick look, and though the woman's face was carefully expressionless, she sensed something was wrong.

"It's fine," said Tracey. "I'm okay from here. Thanks for the lift."

But the housekeeper was walking up the drive anyway, not even pretending to wait for her, and as Tracey began to panic, the housekeeper pressed the doorbell.

"I have a key to the back," Tracey protested. "There's no need to ring. I'm fine now. Okay? Bye."

But neither of them moved, and they were both standing there, watching each other when the front door opened and Tracey's father, looking quizzical, peered out.

"Hello?" he said, concerned as soon as he saw the dour look on the housekeeper's face. "Tracey, what's going on?"

"Nothing," Tracey tried. "This lady just gave me a ride home. That's all."

"Yeah?" said her father, turning to look at the housekeeper. "That was kind of you."

"It seems," said the housekeeper, "that you have a problem. But don't worry. I'm here to help."

And without another word, she stepped past Tracey's father and into the house.

The next few moments were a blur of confusion and panic in Tracey's head, as she watched her parents' awkward politeness turn into bafflement and indignation at what the housekeeper had to say.

"Ghosts?" said Tracey's father. "Like *spooks and spectres* ghosts? I'm sorry, and I'm sure you're trying to be nice, but that's bonkers."

The whole family was sitting in the lounge with the housekeeper who had announced that her name was Mrs. Nora Macintyre. There was a strange tension in the air and everyone was perching stiffly on the edges of their chairs.

"And you think you've seen something, Tracey?" asked her mother, leaning forward, her face pained. "Why didn't you say something, love?"

Tracey didn't speak. She had, so far, neither confirmed nor denied what Mrs. Macintyre claimed she had confessed at the church, and she did not know what to do. If she lied, said that the housekeeper was delusional or had misunderstood a joke or something, she would have to deal with her anger, and the woman looked formidable. If she admitted it was true, she would get scorn from her dad and anxiety from her mum. Neither would believe her, but would chalk the situation down to different causes.

"Tell 'er, Trace," said her dad, a sigh in his voice. "Tell 'er she got the wrong end o' the stick. You're not seeing ghosts, are you, love?"

Tracey studied the carpet.

"Tracey," said her mum. "Answer your father. What's this all about?"

Tracey closed her eyes and took a long breath.

"The people who lived here," she said. "The people you bought the house from. They had a boy who died.

His room was my room. Sometimes . . ." she paused, still deciding. "Sometimes it's like I can feel him there."

"Oh, Tracey," said her mum, leaning over to hug her.

"You said you saw him," said the housekeeper. "You said he moved things around in your room, that he was trying to talk to you."

"That's just . . ." her father began, opening his hands. "Always has had an overactive imagination has our Trace, isn't that right, love?"

Tracey, whose eyes were wide but bright with unshed tears looked from her father to the housekeeper and nodded once, though it wasn't true and he knew it.

"It sounds to me," said Mrs. Macintyre, "that we are dealing with more than an overactive imagination."

"I think I know my daughter, thanks," said Tracey's father. He was smiling, but it was taking an effort. "I appreciate you bringing the matter to our attention and all, but we'll take it from 'ere."

"You might begin," she said, "by calling the church. Father Edwards might be able to help. Perhaps bless the house."

Mr. Blenkinsop's face clouded.

"There'll be no exorcisms performed on my daughter," he said, standing up, his knuckles clenched.

"I am not suggesting . . ." the housekeeper began, but it was too late.

"Thank you for bringing her home," said Tracey's dad, crisply. "Now, if you don't mind . . ."

Mrs. Macintyre's face hardened still further and she studied the carpet for a long, thoughtful moment before rising slowly to her feet.

Mr. Blenkinsop led the way through to the front door. Mrs. Macintyre gave Tracey one last, knowing look, nodded curtly to her parents, and left.

"Religious busybodies," muttered Tracey's dad as the Triumph pulled away, "bringing their superstitious nonsense into my house. I won't have it. Recruiting, is what it is. Just want us to join their church and give 'em our money. Manipulating a child like that," he added, half to himself, "it's a disgrace."

* * *

"Where's Marsh Lane?" said Preston.

Roarer frowned.

"In town," he said. "Near the railway station. Runs from Roper Hall on Friargate down t' river. What do you want to go there for?"

"Near Avenham Park?"

"Nah. North of Fishergate 'ill," said Roarer, "why?"

"Just curious," Preston answered. He wasn't sure

Roarer would understand his new sympathy for the Bannister Doll. Wasn't sure he understood it himself. She had, after all, killed him. What she could still do to him, he didn't know, but he remembered that awful painting in the library and the swirling hole where its mouth should be, and he thought that he was probably best to ignore any understanding for the girl who had been Dorothy Bannister. He thought of the ghost dogs, their sense of self stripped down to a communal urge to hunt and tear, and of the Brakeman who had forgotten his own name in his attempt to undo the mistakes of his past. The grotesque injustice and cruelty of Dorothy Bannister's death had driven her mad, so that now she was no better than a monster wreaking her wild revenge on anyone who crossed her path. To go after her, to try and convince her that people knew her story and felt sorry for her so she might move on, was beyond hopeful. It was crazy. And dangerous.

"You want to show me?" Preston said.

He had feared he wouldn't be able to get to Marsh Lane because he had never been in life, but he knew the area better than he had expected. He and Roarer went into town down Deepdale Road, then cut along Meadow Street, onto the Ringway and up past the Old Black Bull.

"Isn't there a faster way?" asked Preston.

"Maybe," said Roarer, though he looked over his shoulder uneasily as he said it.

"Where?"

"You can follow the railway line where the Brakeman was all the way to Blackpool Road, then on . . ." he hesitated, "through the Miley Tunnel all the way to Cold Bath Street."

"So why didn't we go that way?" asked Preston, pretending the name of the place meant nothing to him.

Roarer gave him a disbelieving look.

"Why didn't we go through the Miley Tunnel?" he repeated, as if he hadn't heard the question properly. "To Cold Bath Street? No chance. Even the living know to stay out of the Miley Tunnel and not only because they could get hit by a train."

"It's haunted," said Preston, remembering standing in front of the black maw of the place, the soulless, lilting singing in his ears.

"You could say that," said Roarer.

There was something in his eyes Preston hadn't seen before.

"What?" said Preston. "Is it the dogs?"

Roarer recovered something of his old composure and sneered.

"Dogs!" he scoffed. "Nah."

"So what's there?"

Roarer thought for a second then spoke with another shrug and an air of carelessness.

"Used to be springs there," he said. "Ages back. Before the railways. The mill workers could go to wash. Cold baths. When the railways came it were mostly covered over. The tracks run deep, but bits of the line are open to't sky down there. But then it's just tunnel all the way up to Deepdale. Right under 't streets. Houses on top. Shops. Everything."

He was uneasy again, wary of his own fear like it was something lying in wait.

"The baths were there before the railway lines were built?" asked Preston.

"Yeah," said Roarer with studied nonchalance. "Dead old, them. Seventeen 'undreds or summat."

Which meant they would have been there when Dorothy Bannister was beaten to death yards from the House of Correction which had stood close by.

"And the baths are haunted?" asked Preston

Roarer tipped his head on one side and shrugged again.

"Dunno," he said. "Maybe. It's end o't tunnel, innit?"

He looked away as if there was no more to say, but his face was anxious. Preston considered him and a new possibility came hard and clear into his mind.

"Where did you die?" he asked. He couldn't believe he'd never asked before.

"Just leave it, all right?" said Roarer, between gritted teeth. The boy was agitated in ways Preston hadn't seen before.

"What are you scared of?" asked Preston.

There had been the hint of a taunt in his voice and he regretted it immediately. Roarer's eyes were fierce and he took a step forward as if he was going to throw a punch.

"I'm not scared, right?" he said. "I'm not."

But he was, and for the first time he looked, even with all his swagger, like a little boy. Preston felt no disdain for him. In a way he liked him better for it, understood him. Roarer had always seemed so confident, so self-assured. It was there in his voice which was brassy and edged with unapologetic dialect, the way he walked which was wide and cocky like he'd just gotten off a motorcycle. When he stood alone in the street he looked like he owned it or – more accurately – like he'd stolen it and didn't care who knew. Preston had been a little in awe of him but this – this *vulnerability* – made him easier to like. After all, Preston was no tough guy either. No leather jacket would have changed that, even if his parents had let him have it. He frowned thoughtfully, aware that he had made a little discovery about himself, and one he wasn't sure he liked.

"All right," he said. "We won't go that way. But we can't get hit by a train, can we? I mean, we're ghosts. We're dead already. What could happen to us that would be worse than dying?"

He tried to sound casual, tried to hide the dread he felt, willing Roarer to laugh and agree, say that fear was just an old habit and they were beyond the reach of anything that might harm them.

"Told you, didn't I?" said Roarer, surly, avoiding his gaze. "There are worse things than dying."

"Like what?" asked Preston, not wanting to know but needing to ask, remembering the thing which had come out of the painting in the library, the Doll with the sucking maw in the middle of her face . . .

Roarer shrugged.

"People don't know ghosts can kill, but they can. You know that. But it's worse than that. They can find you again after they've killed you."

"Find you and do what?"

"Bad ghosts, right?" said Roarer. "Old and powerful ghosts, I mean. They can do stuff to other ghosts that doesn't make them Sincerely Dead. Sort of traps them here."

"But we're already trapped here," Preston argued.

"We're trapped as ourselves though, aren't we?" said Roarer, defiant. "We're still *us*, right?"

"As opposed to what?" Preston breathed, desperate now. But if Roarer knew any more, he would not say.

"You want to go Marsh Lane or not?" he demanded. Preston nodded.

"Then quit your gabbin' and let's get walkin'," said Roarer, his old self again. Almost.

* * *

Tracey was in disgrace, or that, at least, was how she put it to her friend, Carol Drinkwater. Carol had rallied round – supposedly – to be a shoulder to cry on, but really because she was a glutton for drama of any kind. Tracey was glad of her visit anyway, and not only because she knew her parents would give her some space so long as Carol was around. Though her parents' attitudes to the Macintyre incident were different, they would both file the matter under 'dirty laundry', and neither would be interested in dealing with it in front of Carol. Tracey wasn't sure about confiding in her friend but if doing so gave her a little time away from her mum and dad's cautious inquiries about her welfare and sanity, she'd take it.

"Don't worry Mrs. B," Carol had muttered to Tracey's mother as they climbed the stairs to her room, "I'll keep an eye on her."

Keeping an eye on her turned out to mean that she would sit on the bed and gape at Tracey, hands over her mouth in delighted horror, while Tracey relayed everything that had happened. There was no point in keeping anything secret from Carol, Tracey had decided. She would just whine and beg until Tracey told her the truth, and the cat was already out of the bag. Carol Drinkwater could hardly make it worse, even if she did have a mouth like the Mersey Tunnel.

"And you saw him here?" gasped Carol, staring into the space beside the bed.

Tracey nodded. She had confirmed this four times already.

"Where?" Carol urged.

"Here," said Tracey. "I told you. In this room."

"Where *exactly*?" begged Carol.

"Right there," said Tracey, pointing to the middle of the room. "I was standing at the mirror and he was right there, behind me."

"Oooh," said Carol. "Did you scream? I think I'd have screamed."

"No."

"Was he all covered in blood and stuff?"

"No. He was just there. He didn't really look dead."

"Oooh," said Carol again. "But he *was!* Da, da, *DA!*" she added in a voice that was supposed to sound like movie music. She started laughing uncontrollably and Tracey found herself joining in. "I am so jealous, of course, if I had a boy in my room I'd prefer that he was alive," she giggled.

More giggling ensued at the scale of her lie.

"Look at this," said Tracey, fishing the *Myths and Legends* book out from under her pillow. She didn't want her parents confiscating it for 'giving her ideas.'

Carol was unimpressed, wrinkling her nose at the illustrations and eying the paper binding sceptically, as if she was at a jumble sale and looking to score a bargain. But the pamphlet fell open where the ghost Scout had left it, and she was quickly drawn into the tale of the Bannister Doll. When she got to the part about the ritual used to summon the ghost she looked up, her eyes wide as saucers.

"We should *so* do this," she said.

* * *

The intersection of Marsh Lane and Ladywell Street was silent and nondescript. The road surface was patched, the yellow lines faded. The painted faces of the sorry brick houses, one of which was now a snack bar, was chipped and stained. Only the low walls of shaped stone spoke of something old and stately now long gone.

"What are we looking for?" asked Roarer. He had grown agitated as they had moved into this part of town, and kept fiddling with a flap of skin where his fingers had been. "We don't want to be around here so close to the Miley Tunnel. It isn't safe. This is *her* territory."

"Shhh," said Preston, gazing up and down the darkened streets, listening with dread for the sound of children singing. He saw something, a light which hovered for a moment, then vanished. "What's that?"

He pointed down the street. The two boys kept very still, staring into the night.

"Nothing," said Roarer. "There's nothing. Come on. Let's go."

But then it was back, a prick of light, small and uneven so that even when it was in full view it seemed to flicker.

"A candle," Preston whispered.

"No," whispered Roarer to himself, not in disagreement. It was like he was trying to shut the moment out entirely. Preston felt it too, like cold, like darkness in his heart, his soul, and suddenly he wanted to be anywhere that wasn't this place.

"It's her!" Roarer hissed, gripping Preston's sleeve and pulling at it. He sounded terrified.

The light seemed to hesitate, then started coming towards them, and as it drew nearer they could see a pale figure holding it. It was a girl in a long white dress with an old-fashioned bonnet and large, silvery eyes.

Roarer's grip on Preston's arm tightened.

"It's her!" he gasped again. "It's the Bannister Doll." And then he was gone. One moment Roarer's hand was locked around Preston's wrist, and then he was off and running. Preston, frozen to the spot, could not move, could only stare fixedly ahead at the shape of the girl drifting swiftly towards him, her gaze level. Her eyes locked onto his and she came on as if he was the only thing in the world which she could see.

Preston had no heartbeat so he did not feel it racing. He had no breath, so he did not feel it quicken to shallow, desperate gasps. He had no sweat, so his palms and forehead stayed quite dry. But he felt her approach with a dread that started in the very depths of his soul, and however much he wanted to run after Roarer, he could not move. The decrepit buildings seemed to fall away, fading to black in the night, and there was only the ghost of the young woman, her pale eyes locked onto his, and her mouth opening. Preston's terror mounted, but even now he felt a wild impulse to force it down, to master his fear just long enough to ask the question which burned in his mind.

Why me?

The girl drifted closer and Preston's hands rose up in front of him in a vague and pointless gesture of defence, fingers splayed to catch the terrible hands which had once before reached into his chest and closed about his heart.

And yet.

As she came close, he was less sure. Her mouth was opening and closing as if she was trying to speak, and the eyes he had thought were fixed with hatred now looked merely desperate and earnest. Indeed, she looked like neither the figure in the painting nor the thing which had attacked him, and there was none of that dark, shifting malice behind her eyes.

With a great effort of will, Preston looked down. She was not barefoot, but wore tiny leather shoes with buckles and woollen stockings. *She's a shape-shifter*, he reminded himself, but even as the thought formed in his head it felt wrong. The thing from the library had exuded a desire to hurt, to consume, which he was sure he would have felt no matter what it looked like. This was quite different.

Dorothy Bannister stopped inches in front of him but she did not extend her hands. Her mouth was still moving soundlessly. She raised the fluttering candle and half turned as if hoping there might be someone else on hand who could hear her. As she did so Preston glimpsed the back of her bloody, misshapen head.

He stepped back, aghast, and she – as if remembering his presence again – turned to him again. He still couldn't hear her, and she shed no actual tears, but he was sure she was sobbing now.

In a moment his fear melted and he felt only pity. On impulse he reached out quickly and seized her trembling wrists. She was cold, but quite solid, and his touch did something to her. She writhed for a second, as if a current of electricity had passed through her, and her hair and the fabric of her dress stirred, though Preston felt no breeze. Then, without warning she spoke. Or rather, she continued to speak, but now, for reasons he could not explain, he could hear her.

"I cannot find him," she wailed. "I have searched and searched these many nights, but I cannot find him. I have to explain but he is not here and . . ."

"Who?" Preston inserted. "Who isn't here?"

Her eyes flickered like her candle, and a look of surprise lodged in her face.

"You can hear me?" she said.

"Yes," said Preston.

"No one ever hears me," she said, still confused, her voice heavy with old sorrow.

"I can," said Preston, still holding her hands. Her skin was bluish, even in the candle light. "Who are you looking for?"

"My father!" she exclaimed. "Have you seen him?"

"Are you . . . ?" Preston faltered. "Are you Dolly Bannister?"

Her eyes narrowed and her chin tipped upwards slightly as if she was offended.

"Dorothy," she said, considering his hands as if about to order that he release her. The girl had been dead far longer than Roarer or the Brakeman. Preston could see it in her clothes.

He held on, and at last her gaze returned to his face.

"Your father is . . ." he hesitated. It had not occurred to him that he would be able to speak to her and he realised that he did not know what to say. Her father was a monster, a savage, self-righteous prig whose crime . . .

He caught himself. That wasn't going to help.

"Your father is sorry," he said. The girl stared at him.

"Father?"

"He is very sorry for what he did," said Preston, speaking slowly, trying not to look away as he pushed down the horror and grief that threatened to overwhelm him. "He knows that doesn't excuse it, can never make it right, but he is desperately sorry. He did a terrible thing. The worst thing . . ." He hesitated, then tried again. "The worst thing any father could ever do, and he knows it. He will not ask forgiveness because he knows he does not deserve it, but he wants you to know how sorry he is. It was a kind of madness. He sees that now. He is miserable with grief and guilt, ruined by it, but most of all he wants you to know . . . to know that he loved you and is sorry."

The girl's face had changed completely. The earnestness was gone, the frustration and desperation likewise. Now there was only a strange poignancy in her eyes, a sadness which was almost a smile of relief and understanding. She slid the hand without the candle from Preston's and placed it over her mouth as if she was trying to hold in some tremendous emotional rush, and then, astonishingly, Preston saw tears in her eyes.

Real tears that shone wet in the candlelight as they broke from her lashes and coursed down her cheeks.

"You never hurt anyone, did you?" he said: a statement, not a question. "Not me, not Roarer, not anyone else, not even by accident. It was someone else."

Her perplexed eyes held his for a moment, then she shook her head, still smiling softly. Preston's heart sank. He had been sure it was her, had been sure that confronting her would bring him the kind of peace he seemed to have brought her.

Because there was no doubt about that. The candle was burning as strong as ever, but the girl was starting to fade, and behind her the bricked-up doorway of a simple house had flickered into an oaken door studded with iron nails. She backed away, her eyes still on him, smiling and nodding, and whispering her thanks.

"Wait!" said Preston. "Is it true that a ghost can step into their own past? Could a ghost change their future, avoid getting – you know – killed . . . ?"

But the girl merely looked perplexed and Preston felt sure he would get nothing more from her.

Then, just as she reached the door, she gave him a long, thoughtful look, and said, "Find Margaret Banks."

"Who?" Preston asked.

But the door behind her had begun to open and, just

as she was stepping through it, she blew out the candle and was gone.

Preston was alone.

CHAPTER 10

That it had not been the Doll who had killed him after all unsettled Preston, and though he felt a sense of achievement in aiding the ghost's escape from her final moments of frantic confusion, he found he was scared. Whatever had killed him, whatever had then hunted him at the Harris library was still out there and he was no nearer to understanding who or what it was, why it had come after him, or when he might encounter it again. He had been so sure it was the Doll, though now he thought about it, the Doll had never been anything to him but a fractured set of ideas born out of his own fear. He was still afraid, and he knew from that day in the library when he had first crossed into the world of the living that it – whatever it was – was not yet done with him. He found himself constantly listening for the sound of children singing.

Beneath his fear, however, he found that his sympathy for Dolly Bannister – misunderstood, cut down before she could even really be called an adult – spoke to his own predicament. He thought of all the things he would never be able to do, the life he would never experience. He thought of the girl who now lived in the room which had been his, a person from whom he was separated by death itself, a girl he would never truly meet. He might see her again, but he would never be in the same space as her, not really, not like he had been with Yvonne when he might, if he had been braver, leaned into those perfect lips, slid a hand around her waist . . . If only he had been more like Roarer, cockier, tougher, the kind of boy girls noticed, the kind who could – more to the point – hold their attention thereafter.

But he was trapped like a goldfish in a bowl, swimming around the same lightless landscape of the last beatings of his heart, a world in which there would be no sunrise, no kisses, no change of any kind.

It took ages – hours, days? – to find Roarer, and the boy had developed an uncertain, anxious look. He had climbed onto the top of one of the cemetery's stone gateposts and watched Preston approach sidelong saying nothing. It seemed to Preston that Roarer was choosing this inaccessible perch a lot lately, probably because he knew Preston – who had never been one for scaling public buildings in life – couldn't join him there. He crouched at the top like a sullen gargoyle, staring at his hands and saying nothing.

"Who is Margaret Banks?" Preston asked.

Roarer shrugged.

"Never 'eard of her," he said.

"I set Dolly Bannister free," said Preston. "It was her. The real her, but I set her free."

"Bully for you," said Roarer, not looking at him.

"What's your problem?" Preston snapped.

"Ain't got a problem, 'cept you, Mr. Ghost Saviour."

"What did I do?"

"Causin' trouble, you are," said Roarer, shooting him a dark look. "Going where you shouldn't. Gonna get us both killed for good and all."

Preston glared back, but when the other boy wouldn't say anything else, he lost his temper and said what he felt he had been keeping to himself for ages.

"You call yourself Roarer," he scoffed, "and you say that you're your own man and not afraid of anything. But other ghosts terrify you! When the Doll came you ran! She was just a girl who barely even knew she was dead and you ran from her like those dogs were back and . . ."

"It was her," Roarer spat, not looking at Preston.

"What was?"

"The one that . . ." he paused, and looked out across the darkness of Ribbleton Avenue to the horse chestnuts that loomed over the hedge on the other side. "The one that got me."

Preston's sneer dried up.

"You think she was the one who killed you?" he said.

"Yes," said Roarer, looking down through the gloom at him now. "In the Miley Tunnel."

"It wasn't," said Preston.

"That's what you say."

"Did it look like a girl? A *single* girl?"

Roarer hesitated but he didn't say anything.

"Maybe it kind of looked like her, or said it was her, but you could feel something else, couldn't you?" said Preston. "More than one face, maybe, but only one pair of feet."

Roarer looked up at that.

"Bare feet, right?" said Preston.

"It were the Doll. It said . . ."

"No. It lies."

There was a long and loaded silence between them, and then Roarer said, "I thought . . . I thought it were the Doll." He sounded unsure.

"I thought the same thing," said Preston. "The one who got me. I thought it was her. Right down there," he

added, pointing towards the horse chestnuts and down
Stuart Road to where the railway line ran behind the trees.
"That's where it happened. I thought it was her. It wasn't.
There's something else. I don't know what it is – or was
– but it feeds on fear. Sadness too, I think. That's why it
does what it does."

Roarer scowled but said nothing.

"Don't matter," he said, at last.

"What?" said Preston.

"We're still here aren't we? Still dead. Don't matter
what got us."

"What if it's still out there looking for other kids –
living kids? What if it kills more."

"Great," said Roarer, fiercely. "Maybe they'll become
ghosts like us and we'll have more people to play with.
Frankly, you're getting boring."

And with that he slipped effortlessly down the wrought
iron gate and walked into the oppressive blackness of the
graveyard.

Stung, Preston muttered a curse, then did what he
always did when he felt lost and alone. He went home,
telling himself he was better off by himself anyway.

Roarer knew nothing about Dolly Bannister or
Margaret Banks. Roarer knew nothing about anything.

Stupid Roarer. Didn't even know how long he'd been dead.

Ran from poor little Dolly Bannister like every demon in Hell was after him.

Preston grinned to himself, a hard, satisfied grin that made him feel a little less alone, a little less discarded, and he focussed on the name the Bannister girl had given him.

She had to be a ghost, this Margaret Banks, but if so she was one Preston had not come across in his wanderings around town. But then there were still places he had avoided. Cold Bath Street and the western mouth of the Miley Tunnel had been no more than a couple of streets away from the site haunted by the spirit of Dolly Bannister. That couldn't be a coincidence.

Roarer was afraid to go near the place, and Preston recalled that even in life the tunnel had an evil reputation. He thought of the children singing from the darkness inside and wondered if one of them had once been Margaret Banks.

That possibility woke a cold dread in his chest which spread through him like mist. Dolly Bannister had told him to find this Margaret Banks, but if she was in there, if she was one of them, he didn't think he had the strength. And even if Dolly had been right, there was no reason to think he would be able to communicate with the girl now, not if she had become part of the barefoot monster which had killed him. That thing, whatever it was, could only hate, could only seek pain, sadness, desolation. There could be no hope for him in encountering that.

He needed to know more about Margaret Banks. There might be something about her in the *Myths and Legends* book, and that meant going up once more to the room that had been his and crossing into the living present. He wondered if the girl would be there, feeling again that confused pang of anticipation and panic, wondering too if the book had become an excuse to see her.

It was perhaps predictable, given how few people he saw these days, that her image had impressed itself on his memory, but it seemed to him curious that her face was so clear in his mind, her smile, her knowing eyes, the tangle of her chestnut hair. She was, he suspected, not as beautiful as Janet Littlechild, not the way the world would see it anyway, but there was a spark of personality in her face that came off her like heat, like electricity. She was clever, he thought. He felt it. She would argue with him, fight her corner, and the thought that he would never actually get to hear her do so quelled his smile, suddenly seeming like a terrible absence, a blank and empty space where he should have had a life.

* * *

Preston cut through Moorfield Drive to the back door, but as soon as he got inside he sensed something was wrong. The house looked and felt the same, unchanged from the moment he had died, but he felt a half-presence, like someone watching him. He searched the downstairs and, finding nothing, shrugged the feeling off, but up in his room it came back. He stood and looked out into the street past the pear tree.

Something was out there, something big and awkward, standing perfectly still between the gateposts on small bare feet, something gazing rapt up at him. It was quite still in the dark, little more than a shadow, but it oozed malevolence. Preston couldn't see its face, but he didn't need to, and besides the thing at the gate could look like anything. Eventually the eyes would become fringed, sightless mouths, and then – somehow – they would turn into that gaping vortex swirl which would suck Preston in, or worse.

As he looked he heard the swirl of the old song snaking up to him through the darkness – *"Oh, don't deceive me. Oh never leave me"* – but this time the children's voices were thick and sticky, as if coming from inside something rotten.

Preston ducked hurriedly down below the window ledge, feeling the paralysis of fear seeping into his bones once more, but he forced himself to inch his head up until he could see. It was still there, still cast in total shadow so that its face was invisible but, he felt sure that it was gazing up at the window still, unmoving.

"Early one morning just as the sun was rising . . ." crooned the fetid voices below.

Preston dropped down again, the sense of dread swelling inside him. He may be safe in the house or he may not. He could only go to places he had been in life but he sensed that the thing at the gate was more powerful than he was, could do things Preston would never master. He had to get away but he daren't step outside. There was, he thought, the living present, which was where he had intended to go in the first place. It had, after all, worked for him in the library . . .

He closed his eyes and focused.

When he opened them it was still dark, but the colours of the walls had changed. He stood up and there was the girl asleep in his – or rather her – bed, the *Myths and Legends* book half protruding from beneath her pillow. The curtains were closed, but the singing had stopped. He had – for the moment – escaped.

He considered the girl, wondering if she was pretty and, angling his head slightly, decided that she was. It was an ordinary prettiness, not like the girls on television, but that didn't make it any less powerful, and in sleep she was, strangely, undeniably beautiful. There was even that crackle of personality about her in sleep.

He watched the way the duvet moulded to her body and when she rolled absently onto her back the cover shifted, revealing a few inches of bare skin. Preston blinked, embarrassed, but nothing happened. Of course it didn't. In life this would have been a relief, but here and now, it only served to remind him what he was, what he could not have.

The girl's eyes opened. They widened in a flash and she sat up, hugging the duvet to her chest.

Preston took a step backwards, but she was gesturing wildly, mouthing words he couldn't hear and fishing for another book from a drawer in the cabinet by her bed. She pulled it out, checking that the door to the room was closed, and thumbed through pages of what looked to be hand-written statements and questions in block capitals. Finding the page she wanted she turned the book around and brandished the question in front of him.

You are Preston Oldcorn? It said.

Preston stared, blinked, and nodded once. The girl permitted the flash of a smile – and there it was again, that spark of something special that, if he had a pulse, would have quickened it – before earnestly returning to the book and turning the page.

You lived here? It said.

Again Preston nodded.

She flipped to the back of the book and there, triple underlined, was a joyous burst of coloured pen.

I knew it! It said. *I told the house keeper at Blessed Sacrament church. I knew it!*

Preston stared at the words. The house keeper? That was Mrs. Macintyre. He smiled, and she turned to another page.

I met you, it said. *Once, when you were alive. On the street. You didn't speak.*

Preston looked down, abashed. Even in this surreal conversation he felt his old embarrassment rising and he could do nothing but frame a vague, apologetic shrug.

The girl rolled her eyes then hesitated thoughtfully and chose a different page. When she showed it to him, her face was cautious, watchful.

Are you dangerous?

Preston shook his head, glad of something he could answer clearly and with certainty.

The girl sat back, smiling, then turned to another page. She showed it.

My name is Tracey Blenkinsop* it said at the top. Preston leaned in to read the smaller print at the bottom. **The stupidest name in the world.*

Preston felt a surge of strange delight. He wasn't surprised. He had known she would be like this. He watched her knowing, excited eyes, her lips and, without thinking, he reached out towards her face. A flicker of uncertainty came into her eyes and he realised what he was doing, like he was watching himself from a distance. He stopped, gripped by a wild alarm. The splayed fingers which were moving towards her cheek rearranged themselves until they were pointing at the book under her pillow. For a second, she held his eyes with her own, questioning, and when he just stood there, pointing, she pulled the book out and opened it to the contents page.

Glad of something to do that would stop her from looking at him, Preston motioned for her to turn the page and she did so. There, just before the section on the Bannister Doll, was a brief chapter on the Miley Tunnel. He jabbed at it with his finger and she, perplexed but eager, turned to the page and laid the open book on the bed.

Preston read feverishly, but the extract was all scary lights and noises, nothing of substance. There were references to the sounds of children laughing and screaming in the long dark tunnel between Deepdale and Cold Bath Street, but no names. No talk of singing. He frowned, then stared at Tracey and mouthed the name.

"Margaret Banks."

She frowned back, then took a pen from the cabinet, turned to a blank page in her book, and studied his lips as he said it again. She shook her head and shrugged. He tried it again, but she only looked more frustrated. In the book she scribbled,

Sign it. Like charades.

Preston blinked, then held up two fingers on his right hand.

Two words, wrote Tracey.

Preston dropped one finger.

First word, wrote Tracey.

He tapped two fingers against his left forearm.

Two syllables?

Preston nodded.

One finger against his forearm for the first syllable. He was having to focus harder now just to stay in her presence. He grasped his right ear lobe.

Tracey grinned and wrote *Sounds like*.

Preston mimed holding a steering wheel.

Drive, wrote Tracey. Preston shook his head. *Car!!!*

He nodded and she proceeded to cross out the C and work through the alphabet. He could see her trying each sound in her mouth. When she hit M he pointed at her.

Mar, she wrote. She gave him a dubious look, then reached behind her for a dictionary. With an effort, Preston shook his head. She wouldn't find a girl's name in there and he was running out of time. He motioned earnestly for her to flip back to where she had written her name. He pointed to *Tracey Blenkinsop**, then back at her, then back to where she had written *Mar.*

He saw the realisation in her eyes. She seized the pad, spun it around and wrote *MARGARET* in block capitals.

He nodded and the room slid away from him a little. He caught hold of it again with difficulty and Tracey eased back into focus. If he was alive, he thought, he would be sweating from the effort of staying there. He held up two fingers.

Second word.

The absurdity of the situation struck him, but he ignored it. He mimed counting out money onto the bed and then pushed the imaginary pile across to her.

Pay, she wrote. *Cashier. Buy.*

Preston shook his head, then mimed taking some of his money back. She looked confused. He balled his fists and went through the whole performance again but she just shrugged expansively, her face exasperated. For a moment he just stood there, and he knew he was fading. He fought to hold on but he had already been there far longer than he would have ever managed possible and the exhaustion was overwhelming.

Tracey seemed aware of his struggle and started writing

feverishly. Preston thought she had it, but when she turned the page towards him he just stared. It said,

I know where your parents live. I could show you.

Preston forgot Margaret Banks. For a moment the room swam as if he had been punched and he felt his grip on it slipping, but then he managed to stabilise it once more and nodded, mouthing at her "Yes! Please, yes!"

She smiled again, but Preston knew he couldn't hold on any longer. He raised a hand in farewell but as he half turned he caught a familiar but terrible sound.

Singing.

An old song sung by children but distorted as if they were inside something hollow and dripping. With his last ounce of strength he focused on the curtains which were almost completely closed across the window. There was a crack in the middle. Through it Preston got a glimpse of the driveway below, of the garden which was no longer dominated by the pear tree he knew so well, and to his horror he saw the source of the sound: a hulking figure standing motionless between the gateposts, gazing up. It was barefoot.

Preston collapsed, partly an attempt to duck out of sight, partly the final failing of his grasp on the world of the living. By the time he hit the carpet, the room was his own again. Tracey's world was gone, but the thing at the gates had moved with him and was out there, watching.

It had followed him into her world and back, as if time – which was such a barrier for Preston – meant nothing, that it could slide effortlessly through history, killing as it went. Because there was no doubt in his mind. This was what had killed him. It had looked like the Bannister Doll, but that was an illusion chosen to heighten his terror. If it had a true form, he had just been looking at it, though it was also somehow tied to those twelve dead children, the kids who had been killed by the Brakeman's train and now wandered blindly, singing. It could slide between years, change its appearance, and reach into your chest . . .

"Oh, don't deceive me.
Oh, never leave me . . ."

He hid under the window ledge, knowing it could sense his presence, but hoping – praying, almost – that there was still one thing it could not do.

It could not come inside.

So long as he stayed in the house, he was safe, but he would have to leave eventually, and so – he realised with a thrill of horror – would Tracey.

* * *

Tracey woke the next morning and the word glowed in her mind the moment she opened her eyes.

Bank.

That was what the ghost of Preston Oldcorn had been trying to tell her when he had been miming counting out money. But Bank wasn't a name. *Banks*, however, was. There was a Banks family at her school, and there was a jeweller with the same name on Lune Street that her mother thought was the height of sophistication.

Margaret Banks.

That was what he had been trying to tell her. But why?

She went through the phone book and found half a page of Bankses including two Margarets and an M, but there might be more. Many of the names were listed as Mr. and Mrs. but gave only the man's name. Worse, it occurred to her that Margaret Banks might be a maiden name. If the woman was still alive, she might have a completely different surname now.

But what if she wasn't? The Oldcorn boy had been looking for her in the *Myths and Legends* book, so she must already be dead.

She took the bus into town and returned to the reference library. At first she tried searching through obituaries for 'Banks' but there were too many of them going back too far and there were several Margarets. She could feel the librarian watching her again, his bald head glinting as he peered at her over his horn-rimmed glasses.

"Still chasing after old murders?" he remarked when she approached his desk.

"Local history," she said, decisively. "Could you recommend something?"

The librarian hesitated, mulling the request and deciding to treat it as an olive branch.

"Of what kind?" he asked, leading her through the stacks.

"General," she said, sighing. "I'm not exactly sure what I'm looking for. I have a name, but I don't know why it's significant."

"What's the name?" asked the librarian, fishing a large navy volume from one shelf, then pulling down two more books on either side. "This isn't as good as the Hargreaves book," he said, "but the index is better. It might point you in the right direction."

"Margaret Banks," said Tracey. It felt risky, saying it out loud, but it was also a relief.

The librarian frowned and shook his head.

"Doesn't ring any bells," he said. "Margaret Banks . . . Marge," he tried, musing. "Margie. Maggie." His eyes, which had been half closed opened sharply. "Maggie Banks," he said, almost smiling at something long forgotten which had popped into his head. The smile however, stalled, and the man's eyes widened and he looked unnerved, breathless. "*Maggie*," he said, under his breath, "*leave loose!*"

"What?" asked Tracey.

The librarian seemed to have forgotten her. Suddenly he was all urgency and purpose, though there was a wildness in his face which looked almost like alarm, like fear. He moved quickly through the stacks, tracing the call numbers on the books with his finger, his head tilted to the side so he could read their spines. He was all energy and focus, a man on a mission. Suddenly he stopped, scanned a shelf and drew down a single battered hardcover. He consulted the index, flicked through the pages until he found what he wanted and began to read an extract from what looked like a newspaper called *The Preston Guardian*:

'On the arrival at Deepdale station of the 2:00pm train from Longridge, Henry Whittaker, a wool-stapler of Haslingden, held his hand out of the carriage window to a group of girls who thought that he wished to pass something. Mary Flynn got to him first, but Margaret Banks pushed her to one side and said, "No let me have it". Whether Banks got hold of Whittaker's hand, or he seized hers, is not ascertained. When the train started to move,

Banks walked on by the side of the track but, after a few yards, screamed out, fell, and was run over by the carriages and instantly killed. Some of the girls who had been with the deceased on the platform said that Whittaker held her hand, that he would not let her go, and that she screamed before she dropped between the platform and the carriages and was killed. After the accident Whittaker was arrested and bailed to appear at the Preston inquest.

Mr Banks, the father of the deceased, was also present along with Mr. B. Walmsley, Secretary of the P.L.R. Company and several witnesses. Mary Ann Rush said that the girls had agreed to go to Maudland, but Whittaker took hold of the girl's hand and, when he had done so, the train gave a jerk. The train set off when he got hold of her hand and the witness (Rush) pulled the deceased and said, "Maggie, Maggie, leave loose", but she could not.'

The librarian looked up for a moment but his eyes were far away.

"I read this as a child," he said. "That's what I remembered. Scared the living daylights out of me. Maggie, Maggie, leave loose. It stuck in my head. A sad and terrible thing."

For a moment his eyes seemed to swim, then he cleared his throat and went back to the book.

"The witness saw her going by the side of the train," he read, "and her clothes getting fast, so she turned round, screamed and ran up the steps. The deceased struggled to get away from Whittaker, who was in a carriage about three off the last one.

'Mr Walmesley (representing the company) said: "We knew that the train would be down from Longridge about three o'clock. The gates are open about three minutes before the train arrives, for parties to go to the booking office, so that during that time anyone would be able to get to the platform space". Margaret Kay did not see the deceased put up her hand at all. She saw her go along the train for two or three yards. Her crinoline seemed to catch the train and then she fell. P.C. John Bennett said that he found her lying on the rails. "The train had gone over her head and also one of her legs and arm. She was quite dead at the time. I took her off the rails and into the station tavern and sent for a Doctor". The Coroner, in summing up, pointed out to the Jury that evidence was of a contradictory character and said that if Whittaker got hold of the girl's hand and stuck to it he would be guilty of manslaughter. A verdict of Accidental Death was recorded.'

The librarian stopped and his eyes went to Tracey's. Reading the passage had taken something out of him and he looked pale.

"Might this be what you were looking for?" he asked.

"Yes," she said. "I think almost certainly that was what I was looking for. Thank you. I would never have found it without your help."

He nodded and took a long steadying breath.

"When was that?" asked Tracey.

"December 22nd 1866," he said, consulting the entry. "Three days before Christmas. What a terrible thing."

Tracey nodded, but there was something in the man's face which shocked her. He was still upset by the story, though whether it was the horror of the thing itself or the memory of what it had meant to him as a child, she didn't know. He closed the book and replaced it on the shelf and exhaled, as if suddenly very weary.

"I hope that helps," he said.

"It does," said Tracey.

And before she could stop herself she leaned forward and kissed him quickly on the cheek.

"Thank you," she said.

He touched the spot where she had kissed him and smiled a little sadly. Tracey, feeling herself blushing, fled.

She worried about the tale of Margaret Banks all the next day but said nothing to Carol about the boy's latest appearance and their communication. She wasn't sure why, but she wanted to keep this to herself for now. Carol, however, could talk of little else, including their plan – or rather *her* plan – that they perform the Bannister Doll ritual at the earliest possible opportunity "somewhere seriously spooky." She had consulted the *Myths and Legends* book for details and decided that the best place – and one only a stone's throw from where the Doll had supposedly lived – was an old railway tunnel that was supposed to be the most haunted spot in Preston. She spoke of it with a kind of glee so that Tracey found herself wondering if Carol actually believed in any of it, including what Tracey had told her of her own experience. For Carol it was all just fun; it was creepy and everything, but it was just a bit of a lark. Tracey wondered how she would react to seeing a real ghost, and she experienced a flicker of cruel delight at the thought of her friend's horrified face. A real ghost looming over her shoulder in the wardrobe mirror? That would shut her up. She doused the idea quickly as wrong and unbecoming of a friend, but a part of her couldn't shake the thought that it would be good to remind Carol that there were things in the world that she knew nothing about.

Of course, Tracey hadn't known about them herself

until recently, and the prospect of there being more ghosts than the one she had seen, ghosts of the screaming and clanking chains variety, was sobering. Of course, there was no reason to believe that Carol's little ritual – which was how she had come to think of it – would summon anything at all. She found the idea comforting enough that when Carol's mother called inviting her for a sleepover she was able to sound sufficiently enthusiastic.

"You sure you'll be alright, love?" Tracey's mother asked. "Sandra Drinkwater is nice enough, but I wonder sometimes if she doesn't keep as close an eye on you girls as I would like." She didn't know the half of it and that, of course, was what Carol was banking on. They'd meet up at her house, play conspicuously for a while, then slip out. They'd be back later, of course, but Friday night was Bingo night at the Drinkwater house, and there was a good chance they'd beat her mother home. If Tracey's parents knew, they'd hit the roof, and she probably wouldn't be allowed to visit her friend again. Tracey had already had a close call when Carol had let slip the story of her idiot cousin Gavin who had been caught trying to fence the car he'd nicked to an off-duty copper at the Villa Inn. He'd been inside for a month now.

"Her mum will be around," said Tracey, her eyes carefully in her book. "We'll be fine."

"Hmmm," said her mother, unconvinced. "You sure you don't want to have her over here instead? Your dad and me will leave you be."

"No, mum," said Tracey, a real smile crinkling her lips. "You won't."

Her mother looked like she was going to protest, but thought better of it.

"All right," she said. "But call if you need us to get you. For any reason at all, yeah?"

"Yeah," said Tracey. "Don't worry so much," she added, as if she wasn't glad of it.

She spent an hour in her room as the afternoon wore on, hoping that the ghost boy would return, but he did not and at last she gave up on the idea that she would see him before she had to leave. She took out her exercise book and tore out a sheet on which she had written an address. She wrote 'For Preston' on it, and placed it carefully on her pillow, where the ghost could not fail to see it if he visited her room. She gave it a long, thoughtful look, but then it was time to leave, and she left the note, suddenly unsure of whether she had done the right thing.

CHAPTER 11

Nora Macintyre sponged the soup stain off the old priest's black shirt, her mouth a thin, severe line. He was always doing this. If it wasn't soup it was candle wax which she had to release with brown paper and a hot iron. He had stained so many of the expensive dog collars he had mail ordered that she had taken to making new ones from used Fairy Liquid bottles. If you trimmed them just right so you couldn't see the writing, they slid into the shirt collar perfectly. No one could tell the difference. She sponged a little harder and held the shirt up to the light critically.

Good enough, she thought. She wanted him to be presentable when they visited the Oldcorns, and that was something he couldn't manage by himself. Father Edwards would be sixty-five next month, though he looked older. He wasn't a bad priest, though she thought him fussy, timid and old-fashioned. That last wasn't such a bad thing, she thought, though she missed the old mass forms – the Latin and the incense – far less than she had once expected. But congregations continued to shrink every year. She wondered how much longer the diocese could justify running a church of this size on their meagre offertory collections. And there was a larger concern. With the comfort of the old Latin services gone, what was to attract people now? Church-going had been taken for granted, something assumed and familiar; with the habit gone it took real faith – belief – to draw congregations.

Faith.

Nora Macintyre smiled without humour.

"No one believes in anything anymore," she said aloud.

"What?"

She turned to find the old priest dithering at her elbow.

"Trying to get this stain out," she said. "You ought to use a napkin when you eat."

"Don't mother me, woman," muttered the priest. "Where's my stole?"

"What do you want that for?"

"In case we need to hold a service," said Father Edwards, opening a drawer and rummaging through it.

"What kind of service?" Nora asked, suspicious.

"Any kind," said the priest.

"An exorcism?" said Nora, incredulous. "You aren't performing any exorcisms at the Oldcorns' house. For one thing you aren't qualified."

"A blessing," said the priest. "I want my stole in case I need to bless the house."

"Nonsense!" Nora exclaimed. She was beginning to wish she had never mentioned her meeting with the Blenkinsop girl. "We are paying them a visit, nothing more. We are going to see how they are coping . . ."

"A simple service," the priest continued, waving away her indignation. "Some prayers and a blessing of the house with holy water. If anything more is needed, I'll call the bishop. Ah. There it is."

He drew out the long, folded slip of fabric with the embroidered cross, and pocketed it.

"No," said Nora. She was getting alarmed, though she wasn't sure why. She should have known he would react like this. "I don't want any talk of ghosts or spirits or anything with those people, you hear me, Father?"

"I should at least be prepared," he said.

"Absolutely not," said Nora. "We will not re-open that family's wounds. We just want to see how they are doing. That's what I told them on the telephone. Strictly a pastoral visit. No speculating about . . . anything. We should probably be leaving well enough alone."

The priest turned on her.

"Did you or did you not," he began, sternly, "tell me that a girl you say is a credible witness has seen visions of their son – their *dead* son – several times and that she was trying to locate where his parents currently live?"

"That I did, Father," said Nora, "but . . ."

"And did you or did you not tell me that the girl's family won't have us in the house?"

"Yes, Father."

"Then we must visit the parents of the Oldcorn boy."

"Do you remember what it was like for them?" she shot back. "Do you? We cannot say anything that would put them back there. That's the point! I'm not sure you understand why we're going."

"You don't need to be sure," the priest snapped. "It's not your decision."

He never used to lose his temper like this, Nora thought. It happened all the time now. He was sad and lonely and he could feel death not too far away, and was full of doubts about the achievements and value of his life. She sensed this, though he never said anything explicitly. Quite the contrary. His own doubts and fears seemed to have made him publicly more orthodox, more inflexible, as if he was trying to convince himself. She should have known he would respond like this. It was going to make things worse. She should have gone to see them alone.

"God does not send ghosts," said Father Edwards. "There are two explanations for what the girl says. One is that she is lying or confused. The other is that she is telling the truth. That in turn leads to two possible causes. She is either delusional, and should seek psychiatric help, or she is in contact with a spirit. It could, I suppose, be a soul released from purgatory, but it might just as easily be a demon bent on mischief."

The frankness of his remark, the certainty in his eyes, alarmed her still further.

"Demon?" she gasped. "You don't believe in demons any more than I do."

"What I believe is irrelevant," said Father Edwards.

"Easier to believe in ghosts than demons," said Nora.

"That is your opinion," said the priest. "The church is agnostic on the subject. What is clear is that interaction with ghosts is forbidden and imperils one's immortal soul. This thing the girl has seen looks like the dead Oldcorn boy. If it appears like that to the boy's parents, into what dangers might it lead them, physical or spiritual?" He gave her a long look. "Sometimes the letter of the law is the only form of kindness we are permitted. I'm going to get a candle and some holy water," he said. "Meet me at the car in five minutes."

Nora slammed her hands down on the table so loudly that he started, then stared at her.

"I will meet you in the car," she said, "and when we get there, you will stay in it unless they want to talk to you. Do I make myself quite clear, Father?"

He stared at her, open mouthed.

"I beg your pardon?" he managed.

"I said, do I make myself clear?" she repeated. "And think carefully before you answer, because if you do anything tonight, anything at all, which will remind those people of the grief they have tried to forget, I will end the evening by packing my case. As God is my witness you will not see me again, James. I swear it."

He continued to stare at her, but the hauteur was gone and there was something else in his eyes that was wounded and afraid. She never called him by his first name. For a long moment he said nothing, then looked down, and whispered.

"Yes, Nora," he said. "I'll wait in the car."

As he walked out, Nora Macintyre stood where she was, her eyes turned down to the parquet floor. She was almost trembling with the emotion of the moment, astonished by what she had threatened and how he had responded. In her mind she saw that day in the graveyard, the shadowy figure of the boy who had somehow been there and not there, the boy who had vanished before she had been able to get a good look at him but who she felt sure was Preston Oldcorn.

"Interaction with ghosts is forbidden and imperils one's immortal soul."

And where did that leave her and the old gift – for so she thought it – which she never spoke of but which she had borne ever since she lost her little brother? Was her soul still on the path of grace or were the whispers she had heard in the church, the glimmers of light only she could see down by the old railway lines, the bodiless weeping she sometimes heard at the bottom of her own garden, all signs that for all her prayer, her charity work, her meticulous arrangement of the church flowers and polishing of its endless brass, she too was destined for Hell? How could a God of love permit such a thing? She could not – would not – believe that, but what she put in place of disbelief, she did not know. She smelled the scent of stale incense smoke that saturated the very wood of the sacristy's panelling like old paint, her eyes closed, and for a moment she prayed for strength and guidance. And above all, she prayed that this day would end well for her, for the Oldcorns, even for the dead who had not quite left them.

There was one thing more to do. She moved into the dim hall and called Tracey Blenkinsop's house. Then she took a breath and reached into her purse for her car keys.

Preston slid into the world of the living and immediately lowered himself to the carpet under Tracey's window. Even without trying now he could feel the gentle pressure of the springy fabric beneath his fingers. It would take almost no effort at all for him to pinch the carpet and hold it tight, something he would have not been able to do only days before. Or was it months? And whose months, his or hers?

He pushed himself cautiously up and looked out of the window to the treeless garden and the driveway. There was no choir of ghostly children, no hulking figure between the gateposts, no sense of eyes out there in the late afternoon shadows watching him.

There was also no sign of Tracey. He had not really expected her to be there, but he was disappointed all the same. There was a purple mimeographed copy of a page from a book which she had outlined with red pen. Preston studied it, sure it had been left for him, and read the story of Margaret Banks' terrible death near Maudland – what they came to call Miley, and the tunnel to the place where mill workers had once gone to bathe in the cold spring water before the railway came. Everything pointed there.

He looked over the walls with their garish posters and his eyes fell on the bed. A single chestnut hair lay across her pillow. He reached for it, concentrated so that his fingers were like tweezers, minutely focused, and picked it up, watching it shine briefly as it turned in the light. Something stirred in him, something complicated and unwelcome, something both happy and sad that made him frown. He laid the hair back down, being careful to place it exactly where it had been, and saw the folded piece of paper with his name on it.

He gathered his strength again, and opened it.

It contained only two lines. A street name and number, and, underneath it, the words "Your parents live here now."

* * *

Tracey and Carol watched Mrs. Drinkwater leave the house from Carol's bedroom window, speaking in hushed voices and giggling. Her mother disappeared round the corner, and Carol started.

"Right," she said. "She'll be waiting at the bus stop so we shouldn't go that way. Best to walk along the lines. I nicked a box of Vestas from mi dad," she said, rattling a green matchbox marked with a swan logo, "and a candle from Goretti's."

St. Maria Goretti was Carol's church.

"And," she added, with the air of a magician pulling a rabbit from a hat, "I got this from the cemy."

She unfolded a white handkerchief with her initials embroidered on the corner, revealing a glassy green stone.

"You took it off a grave?" asked Tracey.

"There were loads," said Carol.

"What do we do with it?"

Carol's brows creased.

"Not sure," she said. "The book's a bit light on details. I reckon we light the candle, put the stone on the ground so we can both touch it with one hand and hold hands with the other. Then we call on the Bannister Doll three times and she'll appear to us."

She leered with delight, then threw back her head and laughed.

"This is going to be dead brill," she concluded, rewrapping the stone. "I can't wait to tell Sally Jenkins what we did. You think we'll see anything?"

Tracey doubted it. Despite recent experience she thought the Bannister Doll ritual was rubbish, though there was a good chance Carol would convince herself she'd seen something before the night was out.

"It's getting dark," said Carol. "We should go."

Tracey found herself suddenly very reluctant to leave the house, but she could think of nothing she hadn't already said. Carol always got her way. In her heart Tracey knew that she was brighter than her friend, and it therefore rankled that she always let Carol dictate what they were doing and how they would do it. This ritual thing – stupid though it surely was – was a bad idea. She felt it in her bones. She was just powerless to stop it, and her nod of agreement when Carol got up and made for the door, was touched with humiliation as well as fear.

They walked along the tracks parallel to Ribbleton Avenue and up to Deepdale Road, Carol talking all the way, a single, unbroken monologue which shifted direction as one phrase or idea reminded her of something else. Sometimes she sung snatches of Roxy Music songs. She had a passable voice, but that was less important than her total lack of self-consciousness, and Tracey felt a familiar mixture of envy and contempt for her friend which made her feel small and disloyal, so she joined in. They got through 'Dance Away' and 'Angel Eyes,' but then Carol started singing 'Over You' and Tracey, her embarrassment returning, left her to it. Carol didn't seem to notice.

It was cold. Tracey hugged her coat to her and hoped it wouldn't rain. The sky had been gloomy all day, and now the greyness was becoming full darkness. Neither of them had brought a light except for the pathetic little candle Carol had for the ritual, and the air in the railway cutting felt still and dank. Tracey had walked the lines to Gamull Lane many times, but she'd never gone beyond Cromwell Road, and the unfamiliarity of the place, its eerie silence and the lines stretching ahead of them through the evening unnerved her. The prospect of entering an actual tunnel was bothering her more and more. She tried to think of a reason that they should turn back, but knew Carol would think her childish and pathetic.

At Great George Street they emerged from under a road bridge and there it was. The tunnel mouth and sides were faced with stone but the roof inside was Victorian brick, a rounded tube receding into blackness. Even standing in the opening they could hear the hollow echo of dripping water. A breeze, chill and clammy, came gasping through the tunnel mouth, breathing upon them. Ghosts or no ghosts it was, Tracey thought, a terrible place, gloomy and sinister, a place of tragedy and death. It was no wonder so many awful stories clung to it.

"Ready?" said Carol, gleefully.

No, thought Tracey, suddenly desperate. *And you can see I'm not, but you're going to do it anyway.*

She nodded.

"All right," said Carol. "Here goes."

And they stepped into the darkness.

* * *

Preston found the house without difficulty. He had passed it many times in his parents' car. That they had never expressed any interest in it when he had been alive did not surprise him. It was nondescript. A beige pebbledash bungalow with white trim and a plain door on Heather Grove. It was smaller than the house they had lived in with him, and that surely meant cheaper. But he suspected that the reason they had moved had little to do with cost. They had moved to forget. To start over.

He felt a rush of anger at the thought. He knew that eventually he would be forgotten, but the idea that they might actively try to push him from their minds so soon had not occurred to him.

But then it hadn't been quick. Not for them. It had been two years, maybe more. Perhaps they had tried to stay in Langdale Road until it had become unbearable. Preston wondered which of them had first broached the idea of leaving the house – his house – but pushed the question away before he could answer it.

He moved towards the front door but, since he had never been there in life, could get no further than the gateway. He would have to proceed in what they thought of as the present, his future, except that he did not have a future, only an endless Now.

Nine twenty-two.

He closed his eyes and focused.

The door had been painted. It was green now. His father's choice, probably. Preston looked back into the street, steeling himself for what was about to happen. There were two cars, one parked close to the house, the other on the curb by the road. Neither looked familiar. There was a man in the one by the road.

He was sitting very still and staring ahead. He wore a black shirt whose collar had a blaze of white at the throat. A priest. Preston stared.

It was Father Edwards. Older, for sure, but definitely him.

He watched for a moment, but the priest was not getting out, not moving at all, and Preston's time was short. He pressed against the door, then relaxed the grip of his mind until he could slip through the very wood and into the house beyond.

It was evening and the lights were on. There were no stairs in the hallway, just a passage straight through to a kitchen and dining room. The doors on either side were closed and Preston did not try to open them. He moved down the hallway to the sitting room and found them.

His mother. His father.

They were sitting in those old armchairs he had helped them strip and paint the summer before he died, but the familiarity of the furniture only made the people seem stranger. His mother was hollow-eyed, and her hair which had been brown and long was silvery and hacked savagely short. His father wore glasses Preston had never seen, and looked gaunt and old. Preston held on to his anger with difficulty.

They abandoned me. They moved on.

They were not alone. An older woman was standing in the middle of the room with her back to him. She was solidly built and her hands were moving as if she was speaking. His parents' eyes were locked on her, their expressions awkward, not quite managing to smile. Preston moved, wanting to be close to them, wondering if he could touch them, make them see him, and as he did so he recognised the woman. It was the housekeeper from church: Mrs. Macintyre. That partly explained why Father Edwards was sitting in the car outside, but not really. Something was going on.

He didn't want to think about it. Didn't care.

He just watched his mother, then his father, and the few feet of space between them felt like miles, an unbridgeable chasm through time and space. He took a step towards them, but his mother had risen, smoothing her skirt and looking down as if embarrassed or upset, and then she was moving through a doorway and into a tiny kitchen. Preston followed her without thinking, drifting in her wake like the tail of a kite.

She had stepped out of the room to compose herself. He watched her grip the edge of the Formica counter and take a long steadying breath, her eyes closing briefly, before reaching for the steaming tea pot and the dainty china cup with the roses and the gold rim. That had been her cup for as long as he could remember. She liked the thinness of the porcelain, she said, the fluting against her lower lip.

And suddenly, without warning, Preston was furious with her, with both of them. All his life they had told him what he could do and what he couldn't, kept him to themselves or packed him off to whatever they thought would build his character. They had scowled at his music, the books he bought with his own money, anything that wasn't about school, about 'qualifications' and about those vaguer and more insidious things that were supposed to be healthy for a boy: sport, and Scouts, running around in the 'fresh air' and thinking simple, uncluttered thoughts about the world. They had poked at him for brooding, for always being 'down in the dumps,' for living inside his head. So they had sent him to Scouts and one night, on his way home, almost in sight of his house . . .

It was their fault. He was dead because of them and their stupid ideas about what it was to be a man. And then, when he needed them most, they had left him, bought a new house and moved on. The one thing he couldn't do himself.

It wasn't fair.

He wasn't sure what happened next. He shouted something. Came close enough to his mother as she raised the china cup to her lips that if he had really been in the same space with her she would have felt the heat of his breath on her face as he bellowed his rage. In the same instant his grip on the moment wavered, lost as he was in the torrent of his feelings.

His mother half turned, a look of wild and certain panic in her staring eyes and the cup – the ancient, treasured cup with its pale, milky tea (always weak because that was how she liked it) – fell to the floor, turning once before it exploded wetly on the tiles.

Preston jumped back as if he might be splashed, and something of her shock infected him. He shrank into the corner, holding fast to the room, to his presence in it like he was gripping the chain of an anchor against a surging tide that threatened to wash him away. As the flood eased, he watched as she gazed at the shattered remnants of the tea cup, as her fear turned to puzzlement and then a simpler and more rending sadness.

The crash brought the church woman running to help, but she froze in the doorway and looked not at where his mother was stooping, picking up the pale shards of china and cradling them like a small animal that had died, but at him.

Mrs. Macintyre stared. She could see him. His parents couldn't, but she could.

Slowly, Preston turned to face her, and her shock first expanded, then vanished. Her hand came down and her mouth closed as their eyes met.

His mother was saying something, but he couldn't hear what. She put her foot on the pedal of the bin and its lid flipped up and open to receive the dripping remains of the cup and then, for the first time since she dropped it, she seemed to look around, as if half expecting to see something where Preston stood.

For whatever reason, she didn't. Her eyes moved over him and round the room with its shelves and cupboards until they fell on Mrs. Macintyre who quickly snapped a strained smile into place and locked her eyes on his mother's. Then she was moving aside as his mother rejoined his father in the other room, and though Mrs. Macintyre never looked directly at Preston, he felt her watching him uneasily from the corner of her eye.

A moment later they were gone and he was alone in the kitchen.

His grasp on the moment had stabilised, but he did

not know how much longer he could sustain his presence with them, did not know if he would ever be able to do this again. The thought stilled him and focused his mind like pain. He reached out to the edge of the counter his mother had gripped before she had sensed his presence, before he had terrified her, before he had let his anger reach her, and he forced himself to press until the hard plastic edge felt solid to him for a moment. He grasped it as she had done, feeling her reality, and the place where she now lived without him.

He had already forgotten his anger and did not understand it. They had moved on, but he had left them first, and whatever had happened to him, it had never been their fault. It had felt like relief to blame them, but that was a lie and he knew it.

Limbo, he thought. Neither saved, nor damned, nor even being purged in readiness for heaven. He was nowhere, even in death; he had deserved nothing, earned nothing, left the world without even enough for the bus fare to Hell. He was barely even a memory, and those he had left behind would be better off if they could forget him as entirely as if he had never been born.

The thought settled on him like frost and he felt an empty space in him, where a person might have once been.

Too late now.

Preston let go of the Formica counter, turned and stepped into the sitting room where his parents were with the church woman whose head tilted fractionally as he came in. Her eyes flashed towards him once, then darted away, her face set rigid, but flushed. As Preston watched, her hand trembled slightly and she dug her fingers into the arm of the chair to still it.

He moved towards his parents. They were holding hands now, old, pale hands blotched and veined as he had never seen them before. His mother was weeping openly and his father – his father who Preston had never seen show the slightest feeling for anything – was using his free hand to remove those strange spectacles so he could wipe his eyes with clumsy fingers, his mouth buckling into a grimace, teeth set like they were gripping the reins of some wild thing that was trying to escape. Preston stepped between them. His anger was utterly gone now, and in its place was a chasm of loss and sorrow that reached through his very being.

He remembered that he had scared his mother and started to whisper to himself.

"I'm sorry. It's only me. Preston. I'm still here . . ."

He reached towards his mother's face, his fingers yearning to brush her cheek, but before he could find the necessary focus, something happened. His mother's eyes faltered in their gaze and she said something he could not hear. Preston looked at his father, and he too was staring past him, doubt and uncertainty on his face. They were looking at the church woman.

Preston glanced at Mrs. Macintyre. She was staring directly at him, and she too looked not frightened but stricken with grief. For a moment he just watched her, and something passed between them, something old and complex and exquisitely painful. The housekeeper's lips tightened into the saddest of smiles and a tear ran down her cheek, but when Preston reached once more towards his mother, she shook her head slowly.

If Preston had been able to cry, he would have done so then, and not being able to only emphasised the scale of the gulf between them. He didn't know why the church woman could see him and his parents couldn't, but he knew what that tiny shake of her head meant. It meant, leave them be. It meant, don't make it worse. After all they have gone through, don't torment them with your half-presence. Release them as they have released you.

Preston stared from his mother to his father and back, and furiously, desperately, he felt the truth of what the church woman had told him. They were scarred, his parents, broken by losing him. To return to them now in this wholly inadequate form would only draw out their misery, refine it.

Quite suddenly he was struck by a strange and desperate yearning to be able to smell them, to catch the sweet staleness of the pipe tobacco which clung to his father and the powdery, floral scent of the perfume his mother sometimes brushed through her hair. He knew those aromas so well, but now he found he could no longer recall their quality, their precise shape in his nostrils. He was forgetting, and the wrongness of that, the inestimable sadness of it, was like a lance through his heart.

His hand was still extended to his mother's face. She was speaking again, oblivious to him, and that, he realised, was how it had to be.

"I'm sorry I left," he whispered, knowing no one could hear. "I didn't mean to. And I don't need the jacket. The leather one dad said made me look like a punk. I . . . I just wanted something that would make me stand out, something that would make me tough. I'm not tough though, am I? And the jacket wouldn't change that. So. Anyway," he ended lamely, knowing he could never have said those things if they – or anyone else – had been able to hear him, "it doesn't matter now. I am going to go. There's something I have to do."

He turned to the church woman. He didn't know if she could hear him and mouthed the words carefully.

"Look after them," he said. "And Tracey. I'm going to

find Margaret Banks in the Miley Tunnel. I'm going to go in under the road and walk all the way to Cold Bath Street. I don't suppose I will come out again."

She understood, he thought, and a kind of confused alarm rippled through her face. But before she could respond, he walked out of the room, back the way he had come. He passed through the door and out into the drive, back to the road where the priest sat, waiting to see if he was needed, and then Preston let his grip on the present go. The house changed back, the darkness deepened, the cars vanished, and Preston threw back his head and howled his despair to the night.

For a long moment he just stood there, then he forced himself to take one step, then another. The pain of walking away was almost physical. Almost. He began to run, faster and faster, daring his body to give out, pelting along the street as if the long sprint might finally overtax him and something – whatever it was that was keeping him here – would snap and he would be allowed to die for real. Because he knew now the full weight of what it meant to have no future, no ties to the world of the living which had left him behind. Even his parents had forced themselves to move on, to let him go. But for Preston there was only this, so he ran through the night, swearing, cursing the way his body never tired, the way his breath never got short, the way his palms never got hot and sweaty. He clasped one hand to his chest as he ran, hoping against all he had learned that he would detect a quickening pulse, the evidence of a heartbeat which might finally stop.

Because that was what he wanted now, to die for real. To stop being what he was.

He felt his chest, but there was nothing. His heart was stuck between beats, frozen between moments like his digital watch. He stopped running and bent over, trying to remember what it was like to recover from a hard sprint, but it was a mere gesture. His body felt exactly as it had before. He turned suddenly to the brick wall of a pub and punched hard, once, twice. He heard the bone in his knuckle snap, but he felt nothing, and punched it again, his teeth gritted.

He studied the twisted joint of his right index finger. He tried to move it and it shifted fractionally but it was quite useless. Even now, faced with an eternity without a fully functioning hand, he didn't care. It didn't matter. He wished he was dead. Really dead. Sincerely Dead.

What did the dead know, he wondered – the Sincerely Dead, not those in the maddening no-man's land in which he was caught, but those who had passed on? What did they find waiting for them? Heaven and Hell? Some version of the world? Friends? Family? Nothing at all? Preston wanted to envy them, already did, in a way, but then he supposed it depended on what they found. Perhaps it was different for each person.

Perhaps.

He considered his broken finger again, feeling the way the bone shifted against itself when he moved it with his other hand. He would never have believed that he would miss pain.

His anger spiked again. It had not been the Bannister Doll that did this to him, but something had.

Talk to Margaret Banks, Dorothy had said.

Had it been her? If it wasn't, could she lead him to whoever, or whatever had done this to him. Well, he would find out. He knew where to go. A part of him had always known. The thing which stalked him still, the thing which had killed Roarer had done so in what was still the town's most feared spot: the Miley Tunnel and the old springs of Cold Bath Street. He set his jaws together and began, once again, to run.

* * *

Father Edwards had not spoken on the drive back to the presbytery, but he turned to Nora when he realised that the car was still idling.

"Are you going somewhere?" he asked.

"Yes," said the housekeeper. "An errand I need to run."

For a moment the old priest just nodded thoughtfully, then he said, "Is this about your brother, the one who died when you were little?"

Nora gave him a quick look, shocked. She never talked about Barry. She hadn't even been sure the priest knew about him.

"No," she said, then, after a moment. "Perhaps. I'm not sure."

"You want me to come with you?" he asked. "No holy water," he added quickly, "just . . . for moral support."

She gazed open mouthed at him, tears of gratitude starting unexpectedly in her eyes, but she shook her head.

"No," she said, forcing a smile, and dabbing at her eyes. "Thank you, but no. This is something I have to do by myself."

The priest nodded again and then, even more unexpectedly, took her left hand lightly in his and patted it.

"Is there anything you need?" he asked.

She glanced towards the emergency kit she kept on the back seat, glad of something which took her attention from the soft, papery skin of his hand, and shook her head.

"I have a torch, and," she added, almost as an afterthought, her hand coming to the gold chain around her neck, "my crucifix. I'll be all right."

He gave her hand a fractional squeeze, then opened the car door and climbed out.

"I'll wait up for you," he said.

Curious, she thought, as she reversed the car onto Farringdon Lane and watched the church shrink in her rear-view mirror, that in all the years she had known him, she had never heard him utter those five little words in precisely that sequence.

* * *

Tracey and Carol walked boldly into the tunnel. Carol had started to giggle again, and, as the sheer absurdity of the situation hit home, Tracey nearly did too. But the gloom of the tunnel mouth became an impenetrable blackness only a few yards inside, and though Carol's giggling went up an octave when Tracey took her hand, it stalled quickly thereafter. The echoes carried the laughter on down the tunnel, distorting it so that by the time it faded out entirely it was like it had come from someone else. They took a few faltering steps. The stones between the sleepers crunched underfoot like rat skulls so that Tracey found herself walking almost on tip toes, the side of one foot feeling for the metal edge of the rail as they advanced.

"How far do we go?" she whispered.

Carol waited for the hissing echoes to subside before responding. She checked behind them. They could still see the tunnel mouth back the way they had come, a shrinking grey portal into the night.

"A bit further," said Carol.

The line was not entirely disused. Tracey had checked.

Passenger trains hadn't moved between Preston and Longridge since 1930, but coal, stone, and other goods still made occasional runs, so Tracey was alert for more material dangers than ghosts. Somewhere ahead a curious and unnerving chittering echoed back to them, though whether the sound was animal or mechanical, she couldn't say.

They walked another dozen yards or so, following the slow curve of the track, and the tunnel mouth was lost to them. The darkness became oppressively complete so that Tracey lost all sense of direction. She only knew they were still going the right way because she had not let her foot stop sliding against the iron rail. She closed her eyes tight and found it made no difference at all.

"Let's go back," she said.

She couldn't help it, couldn't stand it any longer. She was glad that Carol could not see her face, because she thought she had tears in her eyes.

"Shhh . . ." said Carol. "Listen."

"I can't hear anything," said Tracey, deliberately not

trying. "Come on. We should go back."

"No," said Carol. "Listen."

And this time Tracey did. And now she really was scared.

Somewhere in the darkness, echoing so that it seemed to come from all around, was a child's voice. A girl. Singing.

CHAPTER 12

"Margaret Banks!" shouted Preston as he ran into the tunnel. He had needed to move into the living present in order to make it over the dark threshold since he had never visited the place in life, though it seemed now that the tunnel was like the nine twenty-two Limbo in which he lived: a black tube that connected other places but was itself a kind of dreadful nowhere full of nothing but featureless, timeless space, and haunted by unspeakable terrors.

If it was Margaret Banks who had killed him, it was because she had died in a terrible accident and the experience had unhinged her mind, made her vengeful and cruel. What she had suffered was awful and unfair, but it did not excuse what she had done to others or to him. She had killed Roarer on this very spot. Preston kept this idea at the front of his mind because it made him angry, and the anger kept all other feelings in check, or at least in the background. Anger – righteous anger, at that – gave him power and purpose, the opposite of the other things bubbling inside his head, the lingering despair, the irrational fear of the place.

He ran on, stumbling over the railway sleepers, pushing deeper under the town, closer and closer to Cold Bath Street.

"Margaret Banks!" he bellowed again. "If you're here, come out!"

He walked briskly forward as he shouted, trailing his wounded hand against the damp and slimy stone of the wall so that he wouldn't lose his way. He couldn't see anything.

And then, without warning, he could.

A pale form ahead of him, flitting around the tunnel. A girl. He hesitated. She was coming towards him.

"Margaret Banks!" he called again.

The laughter stopped, and the girl became quite still.

* * *

"Light the candle!" hissed Tracey.

Carol fumbled in the darkness.

"I dropped it!" she said. She wasn't giggling now. She sounded stricken.

"Don't run," Tracey said. "Keep hold of my hand.

We mustn't split up no matter what. It's probably just kids messing about."

But she didn't believe that. Not for a moment.

"*Oh, don't deceive me,*" sung the child's voice distantly. "*Oh, never leave me.*"

"Wait," said Carol, her voice edged with desperation. "I'll light a match."

Tracey heard the rattle, the first unsuccessful strike, the second, then Carol's sob as the match broke.

"It's OK," said Tracey. "Take your time."

Laughter in the dark. A girl's voice.

Another strike, and then a flare of orange light like a halo around her friend's hand and a whiff of sulphur. For a moment the match was too bright to look at and Tracey winced away. When she looked back, Carol uttered a gasping exclamation and the match went out.

"What?" said Tracey. "What happened?"

"Burned myself," said Carol. She struck another match.

As its light blossomed, Tracey looked away again, and this time she caught the stick of white on the stony railway bed.

The candle.

She stooped to it and snatched it as Carol inched her fingers down the match stalk.

"Here," she said, though she did not let go, and when Carol lit the candle's wick, it was Tracey who held it up.

For a moment the disorientation of the darkness persisted so that the sudden glimmer of the tunnel's walls looked like the sides of a well, and Tracey clutched her friend's hand tighter as if she might fall in. A moment later, the flame stabilised. Tracey took a breath and some of her fear drained away.

Then came the child's laughter again. Closer. Behind them.

* * *

Preston became very still. He was as close to Cold Bath Street as he was likely to get and still be in the tunnel, but he felt sure he had slid out of the living present, drawn by the appearance of the ghost. She was pale and insubstantial and each movement left a blurred trace image in the darkness which faded to nothing, and though it was too dark to see anything behind her, Preston fancied she was translucent. But there was nothing scary about her. She was running, or half running and half floating, drifting with a kind of delighted glee. He couldn't hear anything, but she was clearly laughing. It was not a vengeful or malicious laugh, but exuberant and joyous. She was perhaps his age, clad in a long dark dress with a white petticoat beneath, both standing out from her legs on a hoop, her pale hair tied back. Preston looked deliberately down, checking; on her feet were patent leather shoes. She was moving swiftly towards him, alongside the track itself. Though she seemed aware of his presence, her attention seemed focused above the line beside her, as if there was something she could see that he couldn't, something moving at the same speed she was.

A train, Preston thought. *She can see a train.*

"Margaret!" he called, "Margaret Banks!"

But though her eyes flashed towards him, they moved swiftly back to whatever it was she was watching, and her laughter increased. She was running faster than ever now. Was almost on top of him. And as she came close, she reached up with one pale hand as if trying to catch hold of something on the train only she could see.

* * *

Carol was white and rigid, eyes squeezed shut and hands clamped over her ears. Her friend's sudden terror seemed to calm Tracey, as if Carol was being scared enough for both of them. Tracey held the candle aloft, but there was nothing to see. Only the echoing laughter of the girl and, distantly, something else, a rumbling rhythmic clanking and the sudden shriek of a whistle.

A train.

But not a real train. A memory. A spectre from long ago. And Tracey was suddenly sure that this was not the Bannister Doll. This was something quite different. It was Margaret Banks, and with a shock of apprehension, Tracey, who was dimly aware that the sound of the train was now louder than the laughter, knew what would happen next.

* * *

Preston remembered the way that taking Dorothy Bannister's hand had somehow made him able to hear her. He saw the laughing girl, reaching up to something he couldn't see, and he did what seemed natural. He took a sideways step onto the centre of the line and reached for her hand.

He took hold of it and it was quite solid. Suddenly what had been translucent and pearly white became entirely real and he could hear everything, a gaggle of unseen people, the laughter of children, the roar of a steam locomotive. Somehow, he was on the train, reaching through the window, holding her. And that wasn't all that had changed. The joy in the girl's face stalled. First there was confusion, then there was terror.

She fought to escape him, crying out, and the tunnel echoed with the screams of bystanders he couldn't see.

"Maggie!" someone called. "Maggie, let loose!"

Horrified, Preston tried to release her, but there was something else in the tunnel with them now, something altogether different and dreadful. He couldn't see it, but he felt its presence like dread, and he knew that somehow it was inside him, or he was inside it. Either way, try as he might to release the girl, his hands stayed locked around her wrist, and though she ran faster, trying to keep pace with the train, the outcome was both inevitable and terrible.

But before it came, for a strange second, the girl seemed to be two girls, and while one screamed with wild and terrible panic, the other looked at him levelly and said,

"You."

"No!" shouted Preston. "I just came to speak to you."

"It wasn't my dress," said the girl, "it wasn't Henry Whittaker. It was you."

And then the moment, whatever it had been, was over. The strangely composed face was gone, and there was only the wailing dread drowning out the sound of the locomotive. Preston let go, but something held her still, though it was now outside him and he knew it for the thing which had reached into his chest and stopped his heart. It could look like anything, he knew, but he would always recognise it.

For a moment it was as if Margaret Banks was floating free, and then, with horrible speed she was pulled down from his grasp. He heard her screams as she was dragged under the invisible wheels. And then she was gone.

* * *

The sound was too appalling. The terrified shouts, the shriek of brakes, the screaming whistle, the rush of steam that filled the tunnel with a great bellow. Tracey's composure left her and, with Carol straining in one hand and the guttering candle held up in the other, she began to run, back the way they had come and out. She wasn't certain which way they were going, but it barely mattered. They just had to be somewhere else. Somewhere away from this dreadful place.

And as they ran, Tracey sensed something new, something awful. It wasn't the laughing, screaming girl. It wasn't the Oldcorn boy. It was a presence she hadn't felt before, and it shocked her with the intensity of its rage and malice. It was wild, a yearning, mad hunger to destroy.

It was still singing the old song they had thought was coming from Margaret Banks, though somehow it had several childish voices, all snarling wetly now, "*Oh, don't deceive me, Oh, never leave me . . .*"

Whatever it was, it had seen her.

She couldn't think, couldn't tell where it was. She ran blindly into the darkness and she shouted out her last desperate and unreasoning hope: "Preston! Help us!"

* * *

The sound of his name echoed dimly back to Preston as if he was hearing it over a distant radio. It sounded thin and tinny, and it echoed strangely in the tunnel, but he felt its urgency and he knew the voice.

Strange, he thought, in a second of stillness, *that the thought of her should reach his heart even here. Even now.*

Tracey.

In that moment, everything became clear. Preston knew now why Doll Bannister had sent him to find Margaret Banks, because the thing which had killed him had also killed the girl on the station platform a century before. And now it would kill Tracey. That was what it did, and the fact that he felt something for her, that she had become oddly, inexplicably dear to him, only made it more certain that the thing would go after her. He couldn't say how it knew he cared about her, and didn't know why he was so certain, but he was. She was here and the thing on the train was going to kill her. He knew it like he knew what time his watch would display if he pushed the little button on the side. He knew it as he had once known the sun would rise.

Except that the sun never rose anymore, not for him, and in a moment his mind was made up. He would stand and fight to save Tracey, even if it meant his own destruction or worse.

He closed his eyes and fought to regain the living present.

For once, the change was almost impossible to detect. The tunnel remained unnaturally dark and the gravel beneath his feet felt the same as before, but he knew he had moved in time, and there she was.

Tracey, with another girl who looked frantic with terror, both running away from where Preston stood and towards the entrance . . .

And further in front of them, coming up the line from the distant tunnel mouth was a boy in an old-fashioned coat, swaggering as he walked down the middle of the line, singing to himself.

Preston would have recognized that bad Elvis impression anywhere.

Roarer!

Preston stared at him.

"You said I was scared," said Roarer, pointing, his face a snarling mask of outrage. "You said I didn't dare come here. Well, here I am. What 'ave you got to say about that then?"

"Roarer," Preston sputtered, looking from him to Tracey and back, "you shouldn't be here. Not now."

"You think you're tougher than me?" Roarer scoffed. "You? You're just a kid. Me, I'm a survivor and I ain't 'fraid o' nothing."

But then there was something else, something between Roarer and the girls, a shambling figure moving along the railway line, visible only as a deeper blackness in the gloom. It was like a man but grotesquely oversized like he was wearing a heavy coat over lumpy clothing, or had a dozen bags and packages strapped to his torso. Its feet were small and bare, and it was crooning softly to itself in a low guttural tone.

"Oh, don't deceive me.
Oh, never leave me."

It was moving towards Roarer, getting faster, like a bird of prey making a low, swooping snatch at a scrambling rabbit. Preston called out and Roarer looked up to meet it as Tracey and the other girl shrank back, though what they could actually see, Preston had no idea.

Somehow they were all together in the living present, a feat achieved, Preston was sure, by the power of the shape-shifting spectre, and an awesome power it was too. He felt daunted by it. It wanted them all here together. His courage failed him and he just stared at the thing which was accelerating towards Roarer, until something else caught Preston's attention.

A hard beam of light flashing around the walls of the tunnel from behind Roarer. Someone else was there. It wasn't just the shapeshifting monster, Roarer and the two girls. A woman – not a ghost, a real person – was picking her way through the tunnel with a torch.

In the leaping shadows it was hard to make anything of who it was at first, but then the torch moved up and the woman holding it was suddenly quite clear.

It was Mrs. Macintyre, the housekeeper from church.

She was surveying the scene, her face grim, calling to the two girls, urging them to go to her, eyes locked on the monster.

She could see it. There was no doubt. And that wasn't all she could see. Her eyes met Preston's and held them but then, as she turned, her brows contracted with puzzlement. Her face went through a series of rapid and conflicted emotions, like a sped up film: joy and horror, and grief, all fighting for place in her eyes, her lips, which finally shaped a single word which she called into the tunnel.

"Barry!"

Preston hesitated. Who was Barry?

Roarer tore his gaze from the monster in front of him and stared at the old woman who had appeared to his left. His eyes narrowed and he took a step towards her.

"Nora?"

Even the lumbering monster paused as if caught up in this strange reunion of brother and sister, it hesitated, considering, then chose. It made for the housekeeper and the murder in its heart was clear in the savage lunging strides it made on its little bare feet.

"No!" bellowed Roarer, flinging himself at the thing. It stumbled as Roarer made contact, snarling bear-like, then turned to face him.

"Barry!" shouted the housekeeper again, but Preston was waving at her.

Use the moment he has bought for you, Preston thought. *Get out and take the girls with you.*

He didn't know how she could understand him, but she did. She gave Roarer one last look, wincing as she saw him grapple with the dreadful, bulbous thing in the shadows, then reached out to the girls. Tracey was quite still, but

Carol's eyes were blank, mad with fear. Preston watched as Carol began to run blindly towards where he stood, and then on into the darkness. Nora Macintyre shot one last look back to her brother, then ran after Carol, catching Preston's gaze as she passed.

Roarer cried out in rage and defiance, but the thing was huge, and when it shrugged him off he looked hopelessly small. Its flytrap eyes were swelling, splitting the skin over the nose, until they formed a single widening crack which gaped suddenly, the head becoming a terrible maw, dark and crimson inside. The singing became a confused blur of awful sound, and then the shambling figure's head seemed to dip and twist impossibly as the lower part fell open. The void gaped as wide as the shoulders, like a snake about to ingest an antelope.

Roarer turned wild eyes on Preston but his voice was silenced, and a half second later the creature lunged, a surging pounce that arced down and swallowed Roarer whole, right to his feet, so that the mouth did not close until its lips kissed the ground.

"No!" Preston cried, aghast.

But Roarer was gone.

The creature straightened slowly, its bulk shifting and rippling as it processed its meal. For a long moment it just stood quite still, its hooded eyes watching him, and Preston thought he heard it sigh with something like pleasure.

No, he thought. Not Roarer. Roarer was defiance, and bluster, and a force of life even in death . . .

The thing just stood there, throbbing with contentment and triumph. It watched him, and Preston stared back at it, trying to push down his thoughts about his friend, but he couldn't escape them. Roarer had come to prove a point to Preston, and the boy's death was therefore his fault. But even as that idea tore blackly into Preston's mind, a new thought dawned to push him closer to despair: Roarer wasn't dead. It was worse than that. He had been taken into the thing, consumed but still aware, still thinking, feeling, made a part of it . . .

"*Oh, don't deceive me,*" it sung, through its fetid, greasy smile. "*Oh, never leave me.*"

Before Preston had chance to consider all the dreadful possibilities, the thing turned towards Preston and to where Tracey was cowering at the edge of the tunnel. The sigh came again, louder this time, full of delight and hateful anticipation.

No, thought Preston again. *Not this time.*

He ran at it, swallowing down his dread as his concern for Tracey overpowered his fear of the ghost itself. He cried out, sprinting, his head lowered and struck the thing hard in the side just as it was about to reach her.

For a moment it was solid, and then the impact sent it sprawling. It struggled awkwardly to its feet, its strange bulk swaying and shifting impossibly in the darkness, and then it turned, head lowered, its hands spread like claws. A ghastly light seemed to emanate from the thing, so faint that Preston had not noticed it at first, but now it swelled and flickered like an old gas lamp, bluish and pearly, and by its light Preston saw that its clawed hands were small and thin. But then there were two more reaching out from under the shapeless coat. Then two more.

Preston gasped and took a step back, half stumbling on the railway line, and the barefoot thing with too many hands came closer, weaving drunkenly. Another pair of pale and cruel arms reached out and the coat finally opened completely so that the full horror of the thing was revealed.

They were children. A dozen or more of them. They were packed together, their thin limbs interlocking, toes – those not reaching for the ground at least – clawing for purchase on each other. There were faces all over the thing, pale, terrible faces with drooling mouths and blank, soulless eyes. One of them, Preston saw to his horror, was Roarer, but the boy's confidence, his personality was gone so that he was barely recognisable. They were singing in unison, the same old song, circling back to the beginning at the end of the chorus, a mad, droning, empty sound which spoke of how little consciousness they had. Only the head at the top seemed truly awake. It was pale and its cheeks were so hollow that it was almost skeletal. Its gaze was locked on Preston and its expression was one of undiluted hatred.

Preston took another step back.

"What are you?" he managed.

Every one of those terrible faces stirred. Their lower jaws relaxed as one and a hissing sigh like the release of steam between those vicious, jagged teeth echoed through the tunnel.

"We are the Leech," the mouths said together. "You will join us. But first . . ."

It turned back to Tracey.

* * *

Tracey couldn't run. She turned, dimly aware that Carol had already gone somewhere behind her with the Macintyre woman, but she couldn't identify the true direction in the darkness, and her fear of running the wrong way kept her still. She crouched, staring, half-seeing the spectral struggle playing out in front of her, until one of the figures – the big one, the horrible one which stank of what she could only call evil – seemed to grow solid in front of her eyes. Then it was turning towards her. It came swaying across the track, an appalling grey mass, and behind it . . .

"Preston!"

The boy's eyes moved beyond the shambling horror between them and found hers. Briefly, momentarily, he seemed to smile, though it was a smile that came out of sadness. He was going to do something for her. She could feel it. Something that would cost him everything.

"No!" she yelled.

Her feet struggled to move, grinding into action like the wheels of an ancient locomotive, but picking up speed as she made to meet the bear-like ghost head on. The monster caught something in Preston's eye and it started to turn, so that she saw for the first time that its feet were bare and its head strangely small, not much larger than a child's. For a split second it seemed that it had more arms than was possible. But then the look in its eyes caught her, and the coldness, the loathing, drove everything else from her mind.

Or almost everything.

She instinctively knew that was what it wanted: sorrow and horror. Instead she gave it defiance. Her hand thrust into her pocket and came out with the *Myths and Legends* book.

The monstrous thing did not hesitate. It had turned back and was on her in seconds, reaching into her chest with its small clawed hands. Tracey did not look away. Even in what were surely her last, terrified moments, she summoned what strength she had left and thrust the book at her attacker like a talisman or a blade. In her mind she held the faces of the dead whose stories the book chronicled and she said simply "No."

The Leech felt the stabbing blow and shrank back, confused and surprised. Its strength seemed to quiver and shrink, its certainty failed. The girl had done something to it. She had refused to give the Leech power over her. Somehow she had harnessed the memory of those others the Leech had killed before as if she was standing up for them years after their deaths.

Unexpected.

But merely a token resistance. It had bought her only another moment of life. Now the Leech knew to expect resistance, it would merely put more force into destroying her, and after this momentary delay, its inevitable victory would taste all the sweeter . . .

* * *

Preston wailed in protest and outrage. He hurled himself at the Leech, but this time what had been solid was barely denser than the air around it. He fell into the monster itself, but he felt its shock, so that its very being buckled. It snatched its insubstantial hands from Tracey's body and fought to shrug him out as its form began to coalesce. Anger and confusion coursed through it and for a moment its many heads lost their unity and moaned their vague alarm.

Preston felt a tightening of the Leech's substance, so he

fought and kicked, trying to tear at the thing, and it shook him like a dog worrying at a rat. He clung on, lashing out, squeezing, wrestling as the Leech began to stumble. Airy hands solidified and clawed at him, but Preston hung on and when one strayed to his face he bit down hard until something broke, and the Leech began to roar its fury.

The air around them seemed to shift. Something was happening. They were moving in time and place.

With one last surge of desperation, Preston looked back to where Tracey stood. This, he knew, was goodbye. Even above his fear and the horror of his struggle with the Leech, he wanted to reach for her, to lean in to her face and kiss her on the lips.

Just once.

He turned, and stretched out a hand, but she was too far away, and as the tunnel flickered around them, she faded and was gone.

* * *

They were moving now, not on the Leech's shambling child legs, but on invisible wheels beneath them. They were speeding along ancient rails out of the tunnel and north and east towards Grimsargh and Longridge. It was daylight. The Leech had regrouped, seized Preston, and drawn him into the past, into a moment where the monster felt most secure.

The children's faces were still close to Preston, all but the one atop the monstrous shoulders, but they had relaxed suddenly, becoming separate, lost in their own dreaming thoughts, and the singing had stopped. They smiled and laughed, babbling to themselves, as they picked up speed.

Preston heard the whistle of the engine as if it came from all around them, and the children's faces – now no more than that – responded with something like joy. They were just kids on a day out, delighted by the idea of the train and of being together.

Something stirred in Preston's memory, something the Brakeman had said. His failure to reach the brake of a goods car hurtling down the line from the Longridge quarry. The accident which resulted as the truck loads of stone had smashed into the oncoming passenger train from Deepdale station, a party of children on a school outing. Twelve dead. One survivor, a girl . . .

"Yes," breathed the Leech. "See."

And suddenly, instead of being balled together in an insubstantial body, they were just children on a train. Preston knew that he was seeing it because the Leech's mind had focused, had moved them back in time to something that had truly happened, and for a moment he marvelled at the ghost's awesome power. It was all there, all real: the countryside flashing past, the brass and upholstery in the antique railway carriage, the tang of old pipe smoke in the air. This was no illusion, no memory.

Roarer had been right. Some ghosts really could step back into their own lives. They were actually reliving the past.

And Preston was there as if he was one of them. As if he always had been. Three boys were laughing as they played cards. Two girls on the other side of the aisle, their hair in long, blonde plaits, were whispering and watching them, giggling. Preston stared at them, trying to make sense out of it all, glancing around to take in the children who were seated in chattering groups all along the carriage, as if some of them might be familiar. And to his surprise, one of them was, a girl, several years younger than she had been when he saw her last: Margaret Banks. She was singing absently to herself.

"Early one morning just as the sun was rising . . ."

Preston stared at her, perplexed. There was no doubt it was her. But if he was right that they were reliving the accident which killed the Brakeman, that was a half dozen years before Maggie Banks perished under an altogether different train. What was going on? What had happened to connect those two dreadful days through this girl? It couldn't be a coincidence but . . . Preston's eyes moved from her strange, young face and fell upon another, a boy who sat alone, ignored by the others, staring out of the soot-streaked window.

He was barefoot.

Preston knew that face too. It looked different now, the eyes didn't have that terrible rage, didn't look like they might really be mouths, though they looked red and puffy, but the cheeks had the same hollow, skeletal look. As if in a dream, Preston made his way through the lurching, rattling carriage towards the boy who was also the Leech, or who would be one day.

"Hello," he said. "I'm Preston. Where are we going?"

"To die," said the boy, not looking at him. "We were supposed to be going home after a day trip. There had been a party with cakes and games and ice cream and a brass band. I didn't want to go because I was scared of the train, but my parents said it would be fun. It would be good for me. I would meet other children. They would become my friends and we would play together."

"But they didn't," said Preston.

Was that it? Could it be that simple?

The boy just shook his head.

"What did they do?" asked Preston, trying to sound kind as his mind raced.

"Took my money and my lunch," said the boy, fighting to keep a quaver out of his voice. "Tormented me. Bullied me. Laughed at me. All day. They took my shoes," he said, considering his small, pale feet. "They were new. My mother said they had to last at least a year. I told them, but they threw them out of the train window anyway."

"And then?"

"And then nothing," said the boy. "Then we crash and we die and we never leave. No more party. No more cakes and games. No band. No ice cream. And I am trapped with them forever and can never go home."

"But one survived," said Preston. He nodded towards the child Maggie Banks, who was giggling with her friend.

"For a while," said the boy. "But I got her in the end. We got her."

Preston stared, understanding – even sympathising – struggling with an outraged sense of injustice and fury. The outrage won out.

"So you keep them with you?" he shouted. "You trap them here and you spread death and misery wherever you go because you died disappointed and sad?"

"Oh, don't deceive me," said the boy, flatly. "Oh, never leave me."

"What do you mean?" Preston demanded.

"Grief," said the boy, vaguely. "We feed on it. It keeps us together."

"For what?" Preston yelled back. "For this? To relive your last moments over and over?"

"For revenge," said the boy, and something of the Leech showed now in his eyes. "Revenge on them," he said, nodding at the laughing children who were so busy ignoring him, "and on the living who have everything I don't."

Preston gaped.

"Like me?" he managed. "That's the reason? You killed me because you were jealous that I was alive and you weren't? That's it? All this time I've been looking for a reason you attacked me, and that's it? You killed me because I was alive?"

His voice had risen with shock, with indignation.

"Not just because you were alive," said the boy, his expression souring still further. "Happy. Loved. I could feel it coming off you like perfume. I could smell it on you."

Preston opened his mouth to shout, but the anger dissipated, chilled rather, and he saw the barefoot boy in front of him with a new clarity.

"You're a bully," said Preston, thinking back to Gez Simpson terrifying the boys in his Scout patrol while Preston sat by doing nothing to stop him. "You attack people because you can, because it makes you feel strong.

You were bullied in life and now you've become one yourself, only worse."

The boy rose suddenly, looming over Preston as if he had grown, and the child's eyes were black with hatred. The place, the moment, had made him strong again, and whatever hurt Tracey had managed to do to him had passed.

Preston moved back through the carriage, but the boy came after him, and as he came he swelled, his mouth opening and showing teeth which were large and jagged. His fingers grew long, cruel talons, and his eyes became voids again, spreading across his face, revealing the vortex that Preston remembered from the painting in the library.

"You will not stop us," said the Leech.

Preston took two more hurried steps backwards, but even as he did so he stared the Leech down and said simply, "Yes, I will."

Around him the other children continued to play, oblivious to the monster in their midst. He felt the carriage door at his back and he fought with the handle as the Leech took another menacing step towards him.

It opened, and Preston stepped through, hearing the rush of air and rails beneath him as he crossed into the next coach, this one quite deserted. He ran, and the Leech followed. As Preston struggled to open the next carriage door, he searched desperately for an idea, a plan.

Nothing came to him, and as he moved into the next carriage, he realised two things at once. First, that the Leech was gaining on him, and was already turning the latch on the door he had just come through. Second, he could see through the glass of the door ahead of him, and there was nowhere else to go. This was the last coach. Behind him was only the receding line of track as the train sped through the past and on to destruction.

CHAPTER 13

The Leech was bigger now, still a child, but grey and bloated so that it filled the carriage as it squeezed towards him. The other children had vanished and Preston thought he could see their faces starting to show themselves on its awful form again, heads with gaping mouths turning as if beneath a thin membrane, blank lamp-like eyes gazing at him. Then the hands with their clawed fingers which emerged from the Leech's shuddering bulk, reached for him.

Preston opened the last carriage door and leapt out backwards into the air of a chill evening in 1859.

He was running before he hit the ground, but he still stumbled and weaved. Something in his right leg snapped but he could not feel it, and did not stumble. Not yet. He found that – for the moment at least – a dead sprint kept him on pace with the train, and that was while navigating the sleepers and the gravel. If he could get off the line itself, he might be able to go faster.

He veered left, kept his feet down the embankment, and accelerated onto the path that ran alongside the track. With an effort, he pulled level with the carriage he had jumped from, its clattering, clanking wheels only inches from his legs, then slowly, inexorably, he began to pull away. He caught a terrible glimpse of grey, screeching faces and rows of piranha teeth in the windows as he overtook the last carriage, then resolved to look only ahead. He ran harder than ever, waiting for his legs to give way, dimly aware that somewhere over the roar of the engine there was another sound, distant and irregular. He focused on it and was sure.

It was the baying of hounds.

He risked a glance to his left, and there they were: a pack of ghostly dogs, their mad eyes locked on him. Even at this pace he knew they would catch him. He also knew he couldn't let them slow him down.

Preston had an idea, but to make it work, he had to do more than escape from the Leech: he had to beat the train to the station.

His feet pounded the hard earth of the path. He was level with the rear of the great black, smoke-belching engine itself now. One false step and those massive wheels with their bright rims would suck him under and slice him to nothing. But a few more seconds and he would take the lead. He risked a half glance back. The dogs were closing fast. He didn't have much time. He tore his eyes from them, aware of the surging pistons at his elbow, the coupling rods that shot back and forth as the wheels ate up the track, and ran on, staring fiercely ahead. In his peripheral vision he saw the blackened buffers at the front of the engine, and then he was overtaking it. As he inched ahead of the train, he heard the slavering howls of the dogs. They were almost on him. He steadied his mind, half closing his eyes, knowing that a trip, even a stumble at this point, could be worse than fatal. Right behind his shoulder the great engine snarled and bellowed like the Leech itself, the whistle screamed at him like a tear in the sky, and the loping hounds snapped at his heels, but he kept running. He took two more surging strides then jolted to his right, hop-stepping mid-stride over the rail and into the path of the locomotive.

He kept his balance as he landed on the track bed, straddling the railroad ties as he maintained his long stride. The dogs had blindly given chase, their mad hunger to tear him apart making them oblivious to their own danger as they blundered after him onto the track. He felt at least two snatched away by the massive iron wheels behind him, though he could hear nothing above the rattling roar of the hungry engine. Preston doubted that many of the dogs survived their lunge to catch him, but still had to remind himself that he had not killed them. They were, after all, already dead. He fixed his eyes on the track ahead and kept running, the train hot on his heels like a ravenous steel beast, whistle shrieking again, and inside it, urging it on to its destruction, the Leech.

Preston had still been inside when they passed the Cromwell Road bridge, and had been retreating through the carriages as they went through Gamull Lane and Ribbleton station. From what he could tell – though the scenery was very different – they had just passed Red Scar, where the Courtaulds factory would be, and were moving towards Grimsargh past his old school. He didn't have much time.

What had the book said? A train from the quarry, loaded with Longridge stone, its brakes gone, picking up speed as it hurtled headlong into the passenger service from the town . . .

Preston ran on, staring desperately at the track ahead for a sign of something coming towards them, but could see nothing but fields and trees. He risked a look behind him. The train was falling away. Three of the dogs were

294

keeping pace beside it. He looked ahead again and saw the high gabled roof of a building.

Grimsargh station.

This was the place. Twelve dead. One survivor who would make it into adolescence before the Leech caught up with her and dragged her under the wheels of an altogether different train . . .

Preston tried to find one last ounce of speed, but he was already going flat out. Seconds went by. The station buildings came into view and he saw the end of the platform with its brick steps. He hit them at full speed just as a man with a blond moustache stepped out of the booking office ahead. Preston's foot missed the step and he fell hard.

Bones broke. He felt no pain, but he could not stand. His right leg would not support him. Back the way he had come the passenger train was steaming towards the station. Preston crumpled to the platform, unable to do more than crawl forward. He shouted to the clerk, who was watching the approaching train and checking his watch, but the man didn't seem to hear him.

Or see him.

The ghost train had brought its own reality with it, and Preston was inside that bubble, but he was still a ghost, and the clerk – who was living flesh and blood – had no awareness of him. Preston called again, dragging himself up into an ungainly hobble, but though the clerk was only feet away, he merely studied the watch a moment longer, then pocketed it.

Unable to get closer with his body, unable to reach the man with his voice, Preston strained with his mind as he did when he tried to manifest in the world of the living. His brain screamed with the energy of the thing, and gradually a change came over the clerk's face. The focus of his eyes shifted and he looked first puzzled, then indignant. He asked a question Preston could not hear and Preston could think of nothing better in response than to point up the line towards Longridge.

His face did the rest.

The clerk did a double take over his shoulder, listening hard, looked back to Preston who was shouting and miming, then broke into a jog down the platform towards a network of points and a signal box. He moved cautiously at first, but Preston watched him, and he caught the moment at which the clerk heard the sound of the quarry trains wild approach. The clerk became still for a split second, then moved with greater speed than Preston would have thought possible as he made for the lever which controlled the points.

The passenger train and its ghost-hound escort was

already upon them. It whistled again and then the air was pierced by the shriek of its brakes. Preston looked up the line. The quarry train was tearing into view, freight cars first, barrelling down the track. Escape was impossible. He had failed.

But then, at the last possible moment, the quarry train reached the points and veered hard to the right, into a siding where other cars were waiting. There was a deafening explosion, and hunks of stone flew in every direction, shattering windows and raining down on the platform like a volcanic eruption. The passenger train slid past the detonating cars, still braking hard so that its wheels slid sparking along the rails, but it was well past the station before it came to a keening halt.

Preston sat there, nursing the body he had finally overtaxed, aware that things were happening around him. One of the dogs, some lithe hybrid with a touch of greyhound in it, had been pounding towards him but then simply wasn't there anymore. The clerk who had been watching in stunned horror as the freight cars were reduced to splinters and twisted metal took three steps and then vanished. The trains themselves were melting like the smoke they spewed. Time was catching up on them. The accident had been averted and history was rewriting itself. The dead children were gone and, Preston thought, they had not died, not here at least, not on that terrible day in 1859. They had survived with little more than a scare and the only victim was the Brakeman from the quarry train, whom Preston had already saved in other ways.

As he looked up he saw one of them fading fast before his eyes. It was Roarer, smiling. He was saying something Preston couldn't quite hear over and over. Preston focused on his lips as he had done once with Tracey and thought he caught the words as the boy faded finally from view.

"Nora remembered me."

And then he was gone. It was over.

Except that the Leech was still there.

It was writhing as if in pain, and wailing. It was also shrinking. One by one, the faces which studded its oversized body were disappearing, and its great lumbering form seemed to collapse in on itself until all that remained was that hollow-cheeked, shoeless boy.

He stared around him in shock and his eyes found where Preston lay crumpled on the cracked and overgrown remains of what had once been the station platform. He walked unsteadily towards Preston, as if getting used to his child's body again, and his eyes were full of rage and frustration.

"You!" he whispered. "You did this."

"I saved you," said Preston.

"From what?" demanded the boy. "From power? From being something important? What am I now? A child, mocked and ignored by everyone at school!"

"A living child," Preston said, with a pang of desperate, yearning jealousy. "A boy with a future and a family. You will grow up like the others. You will live a full life."

Something flitted across the boy's face that was almost a smile, but one so dark and bitter that it stopped Preston in his tracks.

"What?" he said.

"You don't understand anything," said the boy. "You saved the others, but I'm still dead."

"What do you mean?" Preston exclaimed. "I prevented the accident. You can't be dead."

"You think they just threw my shoes out of the window?" said the Leech, something of the old intensity coming back into his face. "They opened the door and pretended to push me out back there," he said, nodding down the line. "It was supposed to be a bit of a jolly. A game. But someone pushed too hard. My bare feet slipped and I fell. I tried to catch hold of the door but I wasn't strong enough. Over there." He paused and considered the spot back down the track. Preston just stared, gripped by a new and appalled sense of horror. The other boy just stood there for a moment, remembering, then he continued in a measured voice.

"Moments later, the quarry train killed them all. As it should have. The station workers found my body but assumed I'd somehow been thrown clear by the accident. No one ever realised I was already dead by the time it happened."

Preston stared.

"It was an accident," he managed at last. It was awful, but they did not mean it."

"No, they meant only to terrify me," said the Leech. "But they killed me just the same."

"I'm sorry," said Preston, meaning it.

"You will be," said the boy who had been the Leech. "I will start over, and I will begin with you."

Preston didn't believe him. The boy took another faltering step towards where Preston lay, and then stopped, distracted.

Though the station building had vanished a curious stone gateway had appeared in the night, and between the posts a wrought iron gate swung silently open. For a long moment the two boys merely looked at it.

"That's for you," said Preston. "It's time for you to move on."

"I don't want to," said the boy, and his bravado and menace had gone now. He was afraid.

"You must," said Preston. "If you stay as you are you will do terrible things. Leave now before they start."

"I don't want to," said the boy again. "I *want* to be terrible. I want . . ."

"No, you don't," said Preston. "You think you want to earn your damnation, but that isn't your only choice. You just don't know what else to be, and you're scared."

"I'm not scared," said the boy, suddenly sounding younger than ever, eying the gateway. "But if I was I'd have good cause. You don't know what's through there."

"That's true," said Preston. "But it won't be. It has to be better than this."

"It might be . . . nothing," said the boy, still staring at the gate with dread.

Preston thought for a long moment, then forced himself to his feet.

"Even so," he said. He extended his hand towards the terrified boy. "Together?" He hobbled the remaining distance between them and put his arm around the boy's shoulder.

"I'm scared," said the boy.

"I know," said Preston. "It's all right."

Preston thought of Tracey, whose life he had saved, and of his parents who he would never see again.

"You'll stay with me as we go through?" said the boy.

"As long as I can," said Preston.

The gate was just wide enough.

THE FINAL CHAPTER

Preston lay in the dark. The ground beneath him was damp and hard. He sat up slowly, taking in the hedges of Stuart Road, touching one hand to the graze on his cheek. There was no sign of the boy who had been the Leech, but he hadn't really expected him to be around, not here. This was Preston's private realm of death, no more than a couple of hundred yards from the old railway line which ran through the cutting just beyond the trees. Stuart Road, 15th September 1978, nine twenty-two. He rose, testing his weight on his leg. There was no pain, and the leg seemed solid. His hand too.

He considered it, and as he did so his mind registered something he had not immediately noticed. It was a dragging roar, distant like surf on a faraway beach.

Traffic.

He stood upright, his head inclined to one side, listening. It got louder, a single, swelling engine up on Ribbleton Avenue. He pivoted in time to see it pass, headlights splashing the hedges so that they shone green for a moment.

No. It couldn't be.

His brain raced, and as it did, he began to walk, moving quickly towards Langdale Road. What did the death of the Leech mean? When had it happened? In Preston's present? In Tracey's? Or in the Leech's own, moments after the crash had been averted? Because if it was back then, if the Leech had never lived on to do terrible things . . .

Preston broke into a run. His heart was beating fast as his mind processed the possibilities.

His heart?

He stopped abruptly but before he could put his hand to his chest he knew the truth, could feel it throbbing in his ears as the blood rushed.

History had changed. The Leech had not lived on as a spectre, had not attacked him.

Preston was *alive.*

He raised his left hand and cautiously, gingerly, pressed the display button on the side of his watch.

The dial glowed red, and three square digits appeared.

9:23.

Preston took a long, gasping, sobbing breath, laughing as he felt a tear – a real tear – run down his cheek, then broke into a pelting run down the centre of the street, sprinting for home.

Almost immediately, however, he stopped, one hand clasped to his thumping chest, the other wiping away the errant tear, thinking furiously. Remembering. For a moment the world was as still and quiet as it had been when he had been dead, and then he was moving again, not running now, but walking in long, confident strides, not toward home but back up to Ribbleton Avenue. Though he had longed to be there again, he suddenly realised that home could wait a few more minutes.

At the top of the street he turned left and in moments he could see the car, off-white and pocked with rust. He saw the parents considering the front of the unsatisfactory house and there was . . .

Tracey.

She saw him returning, and the amusement in her eyes flickered, then shifted into something like curiosity.

"Back again?" she said, as soon as he was close enough.

Preston just nodded and smiled so that she looked suddenly self-conscious and a little puzzled.

"What?" she asked. "You look . . . different. You just went round the corner but now you look . . . I don't know."

Preston nodded again, still smiling, then he took another step forward and extended his hand.

"Hi," he said. "I'm Preston."

EPILOGUE

From the *Preston Chronicle*, 16th July, 1859:

From the *Preston Chronicle*, 16th July, 1859:

LIVES LOST ON RUNAWAY WAGON.
BOOKING CLERK PREVENTS CRASH.

A brakeman was on the front wagon, bringing three wagons heavily loaded with stone from the quarry towards Longridge. He attempted to apply the brake to test the velocity of the first wagon, but was unable to produce any effect upon the wheels, and in consequence he jumped to the wagon behind in order to use the brake. Whilst doing so he slipped down between the wagons, fell under the wheels, and was completely torn to pieces.

As the wagons now had no check upon them, they dashed on past Longridge, and the declivity in the line gave them greater speed. When near Grimsargh, a boy observed them coming at a terrific speed, and he at once ran to the booking clerk at Grimsargh station. The clerk immediately went to a siding and changed the points. The wagons then came past the clerk at the rate of sixty miles per hour, ran on the siding and collided with some other wagons. After the crash, the first wagon was smashed to pieces, the second and third wagons were seriously damaged, and the stones they contained were thrown in all directions. Immediately after this had taken place, the usual passenger train from Preston, due at half past six, came up; and, had it not been for the presence of mind of the booking clerk, this train would undoubtedly have crashed and a large number of passengers would have been either killed or dreadfully injured.

As it was, there was only one fatality, a boy of twelve, who was thrown from the train as it attempted to decelerate. His barefoot body was found beside the track, though it was not immediately clear how he had come to fall, and with the only witnesses being children who were quite terrified by their ordeal, a precise account of the tragedy seems unlikely to emerge.

LOSS OF TWO TURKISH STEAMERS
TERRIBLE HELPLESSNESS OF THE CREW

AFTERWORD & ACKNOWLEDGEMENTS

I was born in Preston in 1964 and lived there until I went away to university. Since then, though I have been back from time to time, I have lived mainly elsewhere, and have spent the last thirty years on other continents entirely. The town in this book then is as I remember it from childhood, Preston as it is now being a space which has evolved without me and which, like the protagonist of this story, I glimpse only in snatches when I visit, a place which is somehow less real to me than the past in which I lived. In leaving I became the ghost forgotten by the present, and this book is a kind of love song (conflicted, like all good love songs) to the place where I grew up.

Being a ghost means I had to rely on other people to flesh out some of the details of the place, past and present. I'd like to thank my parents for their research efforts, also Aidan Turner-Bishop who provided extensive insight into the history of Preston, and David Hindle, whose work on the Preston – Longridge railway was similarly invaluable. Old and new friends in Preston have also helped with my memories, Stephen Melling in particular, and I am grateful to them all.

Several of the ghost stories here – particularly the Bannister Doll and the haunting of Miley Tunnel – were in circulation when I was a kid. I've shaped them for my purposes a little, but they are substantially the way they have been passed on over the years.

The Bannister Doll tale is particularly old and seems to have been in circulation by the end of the eighteenth century, though some variants of the story acquired distinctively Victorian embellishments as Preston became one of the powerhouses of the industrial revolution, with all the grim social conditions that accompanied such development. Some versions of the story may predate Henry VIII's destruction of the thirteenth-century Franciscan Friary, the site of which became for a time the infamous House of Correction at the junction of what is now Marsh Lane and Ladywell Street. Much of the land – including Cold Bath Street where you can see down onto the railway line at the point it enters the Maudland end of the Miley Tunnel – is now dominated by the University of Central Lancashire.

The story of the tragic death of 15-year -old mill worker

Margaret Banks (and the uncertainty about whether her death was caused by her clothing or someone inside the train) is a matter of historical record. Placing a younger version of her on the train which narrowly avoided disaster in 1859 is my own invention. Reported ghost sightings of Roman Legionaries are not uncommon in England. Those from the Preston area tend to focus on Avenham Park and Ribchester.

The Preston – Longridge railway, first opened in 1840, converted to steam power eight years later, and shut down in stages in the latter half of the twentieth century. Passenger services on the mainline ended in 1930, the Longridge stretch of the freight line in 1967, the sidings around Cautauld's factory (Red Scar) in 1980, with the final coal service to Deepdale terminated in 1994, by which time the line was operating comparatively infrequently. The Miley (or Maudland) Tunnel is currently closed but still largely intact, and there are talks of a tramway being built on the old rail bed, though those talks have been going on for some time now. For further details on the history of the railroad, see David Hindle's *All Stations to Longridge* (Amberley, 2011) from which I took the extracts from local newspapers. The final paragraph of the epilogue is my own invention, but the rest are authentic.

Special thanks for their comments on early drafts

of the manuscript to Finie Osako, Stacey Glick (agent extraordinaire), Raven Wei, Lauren Harris and Lauren Nicholson. I am especially grateful to Debbie Jane Williams, to Janet Pickering whose artwork has brought the story to life, to Brionee Fenlon, Josh Moorby, Laura Collie, Sam Johnson and all at UCLan who have made this book a reality. It's a special pleasure that the press which brings the story into the world is one which is not just housed in the very location in which much of the story takes place, but one with deep roots in the local community and a true asset to the town.

Since writing the first draft of this book, I have lost my father, Frank Hartley, who loved the town and did his best to serve its people. I offer this story in (inadequate) tribute. Thank you for reading. No ghost, after all, wishes to be entirely forgotten. They hold on to the world all the more desperately as it slips away from them. Writers do the same.

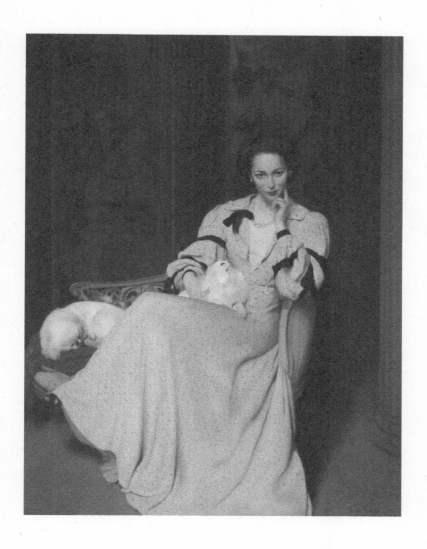

Pauline in the Yellow Dress by James Gunn
featured in the story is available to view at
the Harris Museum, Preston.
www.harrismuseum.org.uk

This book has been illustrated by Janet Pickering
who works under the alias Catie Chocklet.

Website: www.catiechocklet.com
Email: catiechocklet@gmail.com
Instagram: catiechocklet

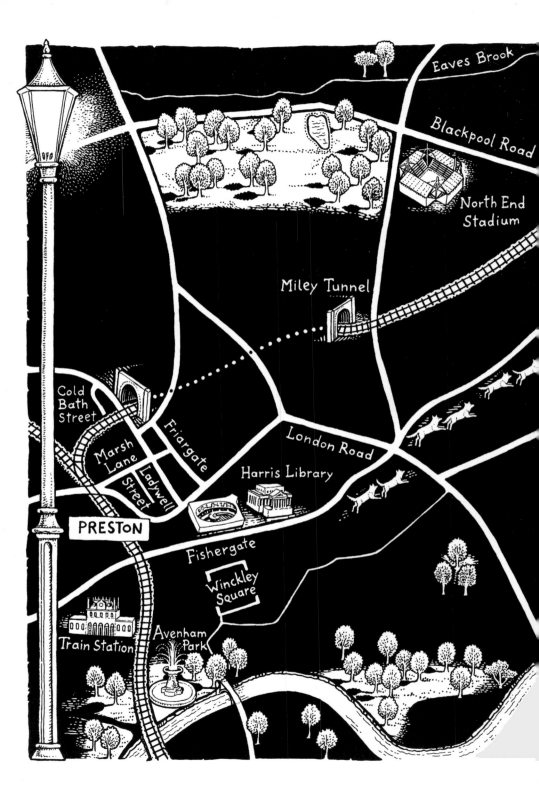